A Case for the Winemaker

A Case for the Winemaker

An Ainsley McGregor Mystery

Candace Havens

TULE
PUBLISHING

Dedication

To Lizzie and Shannon,
thank you for always being there.

Acknowledgments

Thank you to Jane, Meghan, Jenny, Lee, Helen and the rest of the gang at Tule for taking me on and making this such a wonderful process. Thank you for your patience.

To my friends, Shannon and Lizzie and the Bella Lunas, thank you for your support and kindness. I could not traverse this crazy writing world without you.

And to the readers, you guys are so great and follow me where my creative muse takes me. I'm so grateful for you all. You have no idea how much.

Oh, and to my family—no one is luckier than I am to have the kind of support you give me. And love. Always love. Even if it might come with a healthy dose of sarcasm.

Chapter One

"THIS IS HAPPENING." I forced my hands to loosen from the steering wheel. My knuckles were white from nerves, which was silly. This was an exciting day, or at least that's what I kept telling myself. Tomorrow might be the beginning of a new life, or possibly my biggest failure ever.

And trust me, I've had some doozies.

"This isn't just a new job. What if no one shows up for the grand opening? What if those poor people helping my dream come true don't make any money? They deserve to be recognized for their artistic talents, too. If this business is a colossal failure, I'll be laughed out of town.

"If I fail, I. Lose. Everything," I said to George Clooney. When I needed him, he was always there. We'd become close over the past several months. Well, really, since the day we met.

He stared at me in the rearview mirror with his one blue eye and one green eye from his favorite position in the middle of the back seat. Then he cocked his head, leaned forward, and licked from my chin to my eyebrow.

I should have seen it coming. My giant Great Dane was the friendliest dog on earth. I know that sounds boastful, but it's true. He's never met a stranger, much to my chagrin.

"George, we've discussed this. No licking. You're a very large dog, and licking is inappropriate at all times. And most definitely do not lick the customers. It's a good thing you're so handsome."

After grabbing a tissue from my bag and cleaning my face, I peered up at the large Gothic Revival structure that had once been a mill on the end of Sweet River's Main Street. Look next to Quaint Little Town, and Sweet River will be listed. The stone buildings have so many details, and when I saw the mill had a couple of gargoyles on the pointy roof, well, it was a sign. I'm a big fan of weird. And who doesn't love a gargoyle?

After standing abandoned for the last forty years, it was now Bless Your Art, and I was the owner and proprietor, which meant I was either a genius, or doomed.

I wanted to open an art gallery, but the old building with its lime-washed walls and thirty thousand square feet was more than I originally had in mind. After talking to a lot of the local artisans, I realized I needed to think bigger. One-stop shopping for the tourists who came to Sweet River for wine tastings and the many festivals held in the parks behind Main Street. All of my venders either sold out of their homes, or only had booths at those events. This gave them a chance to sell their wares year-round in one spot with, hopefully, a lot of foot traffic.

When I told my brother, who happens to be the sheriff, what I was thinking about doing, I expected him to tell me I was nuts. But all he asked was if I needed help buying the building.

It wasn't easy, because I'm so not rich, but I made it

work.

Between my savings and dirt-cheap Texas real estate, I'd gotten the place for a third less than I'd sold my condo for in Chicago, leaving me enough money to also restore the old farmhouse my grandmother had left me in her will.

My brother and I were raised in Dallas and spent many summers at my grandmother's home. It was an elegant old farmhouse with tons of character, but few modern amenities, like central AC. I'd left Dallas directly after high school and went to the windy city of Chicago for college.

My brother, Greg, had stayed in Texas and worked for the Dallas Police Department, after ten years, he'd moved to Sweet River and we had drifted apart a bit until I decided to move here. I never thought I'd return, but events had conspired to push me back into the safe arms of my small hometown and my family.

Converting the old building for the shop, well, that was costly. I couldn't have done it without the help of my future tenants. The tried-and-true barter system—they'd get free booth space until what I owe them is paid off, and I'd get ten percent of their sales to help cover the cost of utilities and maintenance. It was a bit of a risk, but worth it. They had helped bring my vision to life.

And it was beautiful.

I'd left the lime-washed brick walls inside and out intact. They'd just needed a good power washing. The hundred-year-old hickory floors we'd brought back to life, and we had all new electric, so it was no longer the dark, dank place it was when I'd first walked in. Oh, and new plumbing. All the new pipes had gutted the budget, but we needed kitchen areas for demos, and bathrooms in a place this big were non-negotiable.

It could take hours to meander around all the booths. At least, I hoped that's what people would do, because I'd never been prouder of anything in my life. I've been to a few markets like Faneuil Hall in Boston, but none of them were quite like what we'd created here with the local artists.

George Clooney grunted behind me.

"I know," I said. "It is really beautiful. So much better than even I had imagined."

A tap on the driver's window made me jump.

"Ainsley McGregor, are you going to open our market, so I can finish setting up my booth?" asked Mrs. Whedon. As usual, she was dressed from head to toe in her signature color of avocado green. I sometimes wondered if clothing was still made in that color or if she sewed and knitted them herself. "Or are you going to sit in your car and talk to George all day? You know, that might be why you don't have a decent man in your life. Strange behavior, talking to dogs. Men don't like that sort of thing."

Like I hadn't seen her sweet-talking George when she thought no one was looking.

I gave her a sweet smile. She is kind of fussy, but she has a good heart. A nosy into everyone's business kind of heart. But I adore her when she isn't digging into my love life and why it sucks.

Her words, not mine.

"Good morning, Mrs. Whedon. I'll get George out and unlock the door for you."

I'd been in Sweet River almost a year, and I still didn't

understand why the residents were so interested in my love life. No matter where I went, they felt it perfectly sane to give me relationship advice. I mean they were sweet about it, but just the same. The last thing I needed right now was a man in my life.

Been there. Done that. Have the giraffe tattoo to prove it.

After unlocking the door, I held it open for Mrs. Whedon, whose booth was full of hand-spun yarn divided into colors. She knitted, crocheted, and taught lessons. Her workshop would kick off the series of events—art classes, cooking demos, book clubs—I'd planned, to bring people into the market. I wanted traffic, sure, but I also wanted Bless Your Art to be a hub for creative people in town.

Following her in was my friend Michael, who carried a case of wine. "Thanks again, Ains, for letting me do the wine tastings this week," he said.

"Well, you're engaged to my best friend, so it was kind of a no-brainer." I held the door open for him. "Besides, it kind of goes along with your furniture, and wine will most definitely be good for sales. The more relaxed the customers are, the more they might buy." We'd had to get a special license but in a town this small, it hadn't been that big of a deal. That, and the county clerk was a big fan of Michael's wine.

And hello? Wine is welcome as far as I'm concerned.

"There is that," he said. "Shannon said to put your lunch ticket in early today; they have a big order for one of the women's groups at the First Baptist."

"Good to know." Shannon was the best friend, and she

ran the coffee shop just down the road. Michael had a winery three miles outside of town, but they hoped to get tourists interested enough with the tastings to take a trip out to buy more. He'd won awards, several for the quality, and it was just a matter of time before he hit the big time. Michael's furniture was made out of wine crates, rustic and beautiful in a simple way. There was a reading chair where the arms and base were bookcases that I already had my eye on.

"What's he doing here?" He was glancing out a window at a man I didn't recognize. The guy wore a pinstriped suit and had slicked-back hair. I never trusted a man who used more gel than I do in my hair. And he definitely did not look like a local. He tried the door, and then banged on it. "I'll be back to pick this up in a minute," Michael said as he put the case of wine on the checkout corner and went to the door. Then he went out to say something to the man.

I was busy making sure George settled in on his fancy bed I'd bought him. He had one at the store and one at home. In addition to being the friendliest dog, he was incredibly lazy and picky about where he put his brittle Great Dane bones. Though, he preferred the couch most of the time at home. I made sure his water and food dishes were filled and hidden so they couldn't be seen from the front counter.

George's ears perked up and he turned his gaze in the direction of the front door. I could hear raised voices, but after a few seconds it tapered off.

Then I went to work on the inventory list I had spread out on the front counter. Not the most exciting job, but every item in the store had a number and that was the way we kept track of sales.

The shouting outside escalated. I swear, I wasn't trying to listen, but only a window separated me from them. I angled my head for a better view of the sidewalk out front.

"I told you I wasn't interested and I'm not going to change my mind," Michael yelled angrily at the other man. "Don't ever come around me or my vineyard again. I mean it. You won't like what happens if you do." Michael shoved a finger in the other man's face, something I'd only seen people do on TV, and definitely not anyone as good-natured as Michael.

I'd never seen him so much as raise his voice before. He was honestly one of the kindest, most loving men I'd ever met. When he and Shannon were engaged a few weeks ago, I'd been almost happier for them than they were themselves.

Michael came back in and locked the front door.

"Is everything okay?" I asked, worried.

He shoved a hand through his hair. "Yes, sorry, if you heard that. He's—there aren't really polite words for a guy like that. How about you? Are you doing okay?"

I guess he wants to change the subject.

I shrugged. "A bit nervous about tomorrow. What if we open the doors and no one shows up?"

He laughed. "Ainsley, you've only lived in Sweet River a year, but even you know that everyone has been talking about Bless Your Art since you bought the building. It's the best thing to happen to Main Street in years. It will be great, you'll see. I better get finished setting up."

I blew out a breath and nodded.

He headed to the back.

"Ainsley McGregor, I need help with my boxes," said Mrs. Whedon, "and Maria says she's on the way with her cross-stitch patterns. You really need to give another one of us a key. Then we wouldn't have to bug you all the time." I didn't know why she used my full name every time she said it. Maybe it was a Texas thing, but it was just one of her many quirks. You'd never know from her grouchy outside, but there was a great big mushy heart under that avocado-green track jacket.

Not just because she was sweet to George, but if you love my dog, it's really tough for me to not like you. Besides, he's a great judge of character, and he adored Mrs. Whedon.

"It's no problem at all," I said. "The key is in the door, but I'm happy to help you."

I followed her outside to her pickup truck, which was also green, to grab an armload of boxes, and a loud voice made me look down the sidewalk. The man Michael had been arguing with was yelling at someone on his cell phone, but this end of the conversation wasn't clear, and I couldn't make out what he was saying. When he hung up, he stalked down the street to the coffee shop, opened the door, and walked in.

The man sure was angry about something. And he was taking it out on the people in town, which I just didn't care for. Mess with my people and you mess with me.

I quickly took in the boxes and set them in the booth for Mrs. Whedon. Then I handed Michael the keys. "Can you keep an eye on things? I'm going to run and get some coffee."

Something was off about the screamer, and my curiosity

got the best of me. It usually did. What if the guy had gone there to try and talk to Shannon? Sometimes she was too nice to tell people to take a flying leap. I'm no ogre, but after living in big cities and dealing with grumpy students and faculty at the university where I worked until a year ago, I didn't have such a hard time telling people to bugger off.

I'd learned "bugger" during grad school from one of my professors, who was from Northern England. And yes, maybe I had a crush on him. Hello? British accent?

"George, do you want to come with?"

He opened one eye and put his paw over his nose.

"Well, all right, then. I'll be back in a bit."

I opened the door, and then jumped back as Maria bustled in, her long black hair piled on top of her head and wearing her customary yoga clothes. She was a mom of five, so who knew when she found the time to make beautiful jewelry *and* be a cross-stitching queen. Right now, she was carrying a tower of clear cases full of thread and beads. I wanted to get to the coffee shop, but I also didn't want to be chasing down beads all morning. "Do you need help with those?"

"I've got it. Thanks for getting the door. I nearly dropped it all when some nasty man on his phone ran into me. He was too busy getting red in the face to notice he nearly ran over me. Guys like that should be strung up and—" She blew out a breath. "Sorry. Crazy morning. The kids are a handful today and I am becoming triggered and that just won't work. Remind me again why I have five children?"

"Because you love and adore them, except when they lose

their shoes before school." No one was better at the kid thing than Maria. She managed to be part drill sergeant and Mother Nature all at the same time. Her house was always immaculate, her children well behaved, and she made the most amazing family meals.

But she often wore mismatched shoes, and usually two pair of readers on top of her head at a time and could never find her glasses.

We laughed.

"Got it in one." Maria winked at me.

"I'm running off to get some coffee. Can I get you a chai latte?"

"Yes, please. Dirty. A double. I want a triple, but I also don't want a heart attack from so much espresso. I'm so excited for all of this. I can't believe we open tomorrow. It feels like it's taken forever and has gone so fast at the same time."

"I feel the same way," I said as I headed out. "Can you keep an eye on George for me?"

"Absolutely." Maria waved at my dog with her free hand. "Hello, sweet George."

He grunted, but actually opened one eye, which meant he liked her.

It was a Tuesday morning in November, and the streets of Sweet River were busy. I waved and smiled, as people greeted me. It was so different than Chicago, where people kept to themselves and very seldom said hello to strangers. The weather was mild, and the sun shone over the quaint town. It was truly a storybook kind of place. As long as you don't mind a few quirky folks in your stories.

There were posters on some of the windows featuring the homecoming and fall festival events. I'd honestly liked Chicago a lot, except for a few scary things that had happened there and the winters—I never want to be that cold again—but in Sweet River I felt a part of something. They'd accepted me into the community. Embraced me with a love and support I'd never felt my entire life. Of course, it didn't hurt that my brother and best friend lived here.

I only hoped I didn't fall flat on my face in front of the whole town tomorrow. Everyone was rooting for me and I sensed I'd given a new hope to the community that they hadn't had in a very long time: optimism. And I didn't want to let them down.

The bell over the door of The Perk rang as I stepped inside. The lovely scents of coffee and tea assailed me.

I love coffee. Tea is a close second, but coffee is my drug of choice. We keep a pot always brewing in the break room at the shop, but nothing tastes as good as The Perk's. I've asked Shannon's secret more than once, but she promised it was one she was taking to the grave.

I came around the corner to find that same man who had been bugging Michael talking with Shannon. They were off to the side of the counter by the big espresso machine.

"What can I get you, Ainsley?" asked Ben, who worked the counter and made a mean cup of coffee. "Your regular today?"

I nodded. "Yes, and a double dirty chai latte for Maria. You know how she likes it."

"I do. Double shot of espresso for her. With all those kids, I'd need a quadruple."

He had a point.

"Who's that guy talking to Shannon?"

He frowned. "Don't know, but she's been trying to get rid of him since he walked in the door. I wasn't sure if maybe I should act all tough guy or something. He nearly knocked Maria down when she was turning the corner to go to your place."

Ben was a college freshman who was about six feet tall but probably weighed a hundred and thirty pounds.

Shannon had a fierce look, and I had a feeling the stranger wasn't saying anything nice to her. My friend appeared upset and I wasn't going to let him take advantage of her. I had just enough Chicago in me to go toe-to-toe with the biggest and the baddest.

I called over to her without waiting for a break in their conversation. "Hey, Shannon, I need to talk to you about the lunch order." It was rude of me to butt in, but no way was I letting some guy bully my friends.

She glanced toward me and waved. Maybe she even looked a bit grateful at my interruption. "Be right with you." When she turned back to the man, she made a sharp gesture, clearly telling him to get out.

Ben set about making my coffee, and Shannon came over. "Sorry about that," she said.

"Who is that guy? Michael was arguing with him this morning."

She looked stricken. "Again? He's going to get Michael's blood pressure boiling, and then what am I going to do?" She wiped her hands on the rag she had hanging over her shoulder. "He's no good that one. His company wanted to do some kind of partnership deal with Michael. But Michael thinks there's something fishy going on and that jerk-dude wouldn't open his books and share figures. The guy gives me the creeps, and he's just too slick."

"Ugh."

"Ugh is right."

"I thought the winery was doing well?" I asked.

"Oh, it's great. Michael's just been wanting to branch out into different markets. But he can't do sales and run the place, plus he really likes making the furniture. So, he thought if he partnered with someone who was already distributing—well, you don't want to know all of that."

"Maybe make sure Michael comes down to get you this afternoon when you close the shop. You don't need more harassment."

She smirked. "This isn't Chicago, Ains. And I have four brothers, two of whom are in the NFL. I can hold my own."

"Coffee's up," Ben said. He'd put everything in a carryall for me.

"You nervous about tomorrow?" Shannon asked.

"Yes. I thought by the time I reached this point—"

She reached over and put her hand on mine. "I felt the same way, and it's worked out really well for me. We have more business than we can handle most mornings. You'll be fine."

By the time I returned to the store, almost all of the booths were filled with people putting on the last-minute touches. They each had two walls dividing them from the other spaces, but each one was designed differently. As I stepped up to the counter, which was set a little higher, so I could oversee everything, George raised his head.

I put the cup of whip cream that Ben included with every order on the floor for him.

"Rrrunmm."

I snorted. "Yes. Yum," I said back to my dog. Then I started working on inventory again. It was almost seven hours later when I looked up and realized everyone was gone. The sun was going down, and it wouldn't be long before darkness set in.

"It's six. How about we take a walk before heading home?"

I grabbed George's leash from the hook by the back door to the shop.

It wasn't so much that I walked him, as he did me. I wasn't the best at getting exercise, but that had changed in the days since George came into my life a few months ago. I'd already lost two pounds, and my fat jeans weren't cutting into my waist anymore, so I wasn't complaining.

I'd been eating my feelings for months, so a little exercise wasn't such a bad thing.

Behind Main Street on the north side of our building, was a huge park with the Sweet River running through it. There were walking and bike paths, and it had old-fashioned gaslight-style lamps that made it almost as bright at night as during the day. The sidewalks were bordered by gardens, each tended by a different group. The open, green areas were where many of the town's festivals were held. Handy, since people visiting said events could come through the back entrance into our building. That's why I'd also had a sign painted on the back.

George dragged me toward his favorite tree. But he stopped a few feet away and whined a bit. I hadn't heard him do that before.

"George, I need you to hurry it along, buddy. I don't have time for you to be super picky about the tree. Let's get it done." I kept a firm tone with him when we were outside. But I never yelled. He'd pout for days if I did, and besides, who yells at a dog?

Dumb people.

He growled. He'd never done that, either. And it wasn't at me, it was at whatever was on the ground under the leaves.

A shiver ran through me.

Oh, no. That was my internal scare-dar. My gut always told me when danger was near or when something wasn't quite right. The night I'd been mugged in Chicago, I'd had shivers just a few minutes before. That same sense of dread I'd experienced then slithered through me now.

Whatever was about to happen, I just wanted to run back to the shop and reclaim my happy space.

Think logically. There are no muggers in Sweet River.

The weather was cooler, and creepy crawlies were looking for places to hibernate. I'd watched enough Discovery Channel to know they liked leaves to get warm.

Could it be a snake? There were tons of leaves piled there.

The dog growled again, a deep and sort of mean sound.

"George?" I tugged gently on his leash, encouraging him to back away. "Please," I whispered. Nerves jangled through me. I was scared he might get bitten. "Back away slowly. I don't want whatever is under there to get you."

He grunted and sniffed the ground.

Then he sat and wouldn't budge. He outweighed me by a good sixty or so pounds, depending on how much chocolate I'd eaten the day before.

Stupid dog. The snake was going to strike any second. I pulled him hard, and as I did, his tail swept across the leaves and something popped out. He moved back then.

"Sit, George," I said firmly, as my heart pounded against my chest.

Not a snake.

A hand.

A very dead-looking hand lay in the leaves, and it was attached to an equally dead-looking arm.

Chapter Two

I SAT IN the break room at the back of Bless Your Art, my hands wrapped around a hot cup of tea someone had made me. The police swarmed the park. Greg, my brother, was there, and after talking to me for a few minutes, making sure I was all right—as all right as I could be—he'd gone into sheriff mode.

He told me not to say anything to anyone until he came back for me. The cup rattled as my hands shook again. A bone-chilling cold that no amount of heat would warm had settled in me. But I was alert and focused on everything going on around me. No way was I going to be the victim of another crime and leave justice and investigation to those not involved.

Plus, I'd worked too hard on the grand opening of Bless Your Art and I refused to let everyone down. I needed to figure out exactly what was going on.

The man Michael had been arguing with earlier in the day was dead in the park, part of his head bashed in, and his eyes staring straight ahead.

That image would be burned into my brain for the rest of my life.

No one deserved to go like that. Not even this guy with his jerky attitude and bullying tactics.

"Can I get you anything else?" Maria asked. She'd been down the street at the grocery with her daughter Samantha when they'd seen all the flashing lights. "Tell me what I can do."

I shook my head. There was a dead body. I wouldn't get in the way of my brother's investigation by gossiping about what I'd seen. Besides, talking wasn't something I could even do at the moment.

My mind whirled with questions. Who else did that guy make so mad they wanted to kill him? Was it random? Was there some crazy in town who could possibly endanger all the people I'd come to love over the last year? I couldn't stand the thought of all my friends in mortal danger.

"Girl, I can't believe this happened. The last murder was nearly forty years ago," Maria said.

"Mom," Samantha murmured, "I'm worried about Ms. McGregor. She's just staring straight ahead, and she hasn't blinked in a really long time." Samantha was a freshman at the high school, a book nerd and as kindhearted as her mother.

"She's in shock," Maria said from beside me. "Maybe we should call a doctor or take her to the hospital."

Ugh. Hospitals were awful places, at least for me. The last time I'd been in one was Chicago. I'd woken up there alone and scared after the mugger had hit me so hard with his gun, I had a concussion.

I shook my head. I needed to at least appear normal. I forced myself to blink.

George, who had been leaning into me while I sat in the chair, put his head in my lap and sighed—a deep, comforting sound out of his big barrel chest.

"Good dog," I said with a shaky voice. I cleared my throat. "I'm fine. I—my brother asked me not to say anything until he has a chance to talk to me."

"That's understandable," Maria said. "You were first on the scene, so to speak. I mean, what do I know? Everything I've learned about this sort of thing has been on television. But it makes sense."

I knew a bit more about police work, from what I'd read in books, and the little I'd picked up from Greg after being in town. But I didn't need to give Maria an education in procedure, so I tried to force a smile, but it kind of hurt my face, so I gave up.

There was a knock on the back door, and then it opened. Greg was there.

Tears burned my eyes. It was silly, but he was my big brother. And right then, I needed him, just like I did when we were little, and I'd fallen off my bike and scraped up my knees.

He nodded toward Maria. "Can you guys give us the room?"

"I should get my daughter home," Maria said. "That is, if you're okay."

I cleared my throat again. "I'm fine. Really. As soon as they finish with their questions, I'm locking up and heading home."

She hugged me. "Call us if you need anything."

Another officer walked in the back door, and she didn't bother knocking. "Ains, this is Detective Lucy Pearson," Greg said. "She's going to take your statement. Are you ready?"

I frowned. "Is there a reason you can't do it?" I'd feel much more comfortable talking to my brother than a stranger.

He sat down beside me and took my hand. His were so much bigger. He had all of Dad's tall genes, whereas I'd been lucky to get to five four, thanks to my mom.

"You're my sister, and we want to do this by the book. So, I'll sit here with you, but I need Lucy—I mean, Detective Pearson—to do the interview."

I nodded.

She held out her hand, and I let go of my brother's to shake it. She couldn't have been much older than me, but she had a tough look, as if she'd seen a bit too much of the darkness in the world. It wasn't the look of a small-town cop.

"I'm sorry you had to see that," she said as she sat on the stool across the break room table from me. "I'd appreciate if you could take me through what happened and exactly how you found the body."

I took another deep breath and closed my eyes. I'm lucky in that I have a great memory, which was useful when I worked with students. I haven't forgotten a term paper yet, and I can remember almost every book I've read. I'm able to put things in categories and file them away in their proper place, and I have near-perfect recall. At least, with words.

Perfect too, for an investigation.

I explained about taking George for a walk and his odd reaction. "I'm sorry that his tail disturbed the crime scene. He couldn't help it."

George lifted his head and looked directly at Lucy.

"He's a very large dog." The detective smiled, but then seemed to remember we were talking about a murder and pressed her lips into a thin line before asking the next question. "Do you remember seeing anyone in the vicinity? Anyone who might have been watching?"

I shivered. Could the killer still have been around? Did he or she see me?

There was a hand on my shoulder. "Do you need to stop for a minute?" Greg asked.

"No. I—" Closing my eyes, I willed myself to remember what we'd seen just before George growled. "There was a guy on the bicycle path when we came out of the back of the store. But he was on the far side of the river. I don't remember anyone else around."

"Did you hear anything?" she asked.

I kept my eyes closed. "Just the wind and normal sounds from town. Cars and—" Someone running.

"What?" she asked. "You remember something."

"I didn't see anyone, but I heard footsteps. Someone running behind me. But I was focused on George. He'd started growling, and I'd never heard him do that before. I thought it was a snake or something in the leaves. Some kind of animal. And I was worried about my dog being hurt."

George sighed in my lap, and I rubbed his ears.

"But it was behind me, and I didn't turn. There are always runners on the paths down there. George was growling, and I tried to pull him away. That's when he rustled the leaves and the hand—" I opened my eyes. "The hand sort of popped out. I'll be honest, it didn't register at first."

The cold chill slipped through my body once more. I

wasn't sure I'd ever be warm again. "The wind picked up and blew the leaves off his face, and his eyes were so... I told George to sit. But I think he already was. I might have screamed. I'm kind of sure I did.

"He was just lying there, you know? And then I reached down to see if he had a pulse. Because even though his eyes didn't look so great, maybe he could have still been alive. I just felt like I needed to check. I only touched his wrist. I'm not a nurse. I've never actually taken a pulse. But there was nothing."

I visibly shook this time. Touching that dead man had been one of the toughest things I'd ever done.

"And then what?" she guided me.

"I stepped back and moved George with me, so he wouldn't disturb the body any more than we already had. I pulled out my cell and called Greg. I just stood there. It didn't seem right to leave the body alone. That poor man." Maybe he hadn't been so nice to my friends, but no one deserved to die like that.

Tears burned my eyes, and I sniffed. Greg handed me a tissue from the box on the table.

"You've had a shock," he said. "I'm sorry, Ainsley. So sorry you had to see that." Then he put his arm around me and hugged me. My brother loved me—I've always known that. But we weren't the hugging sort. That squeeze nearly did me in. I had to force myself to blink so that I didn't sob.

"It's okay. I'm fine," I lied. *Or I will be maybe ten or thirty years from now.* When I'd been mugged, the guy hit me in the head with his gun, even after I gave him everything in my purse. Still, it hadn't been as frightening as finding that body.

"I may have a few more questions later about your friends, but I think we've got what we need right now," the detective said.

"I have to talk to her for a minute," my brother said. "I'll meet you outside."

She nodded and then left through the back door.

"Look, Ainsley, I can have one of the guys take you home. You've been through a lot."

I bit my lip. My mind was a confused mess. But I had this overriding feeling of protection for the town I'd come to call home.

"I don't know what to do about opening the market tomorrow," I said. "I can't let all these people down. But it doesn't feel right. A man is dead. I just don't know if we should do this so soon, given what's happened in our backyard tonight."

"I know how important tomorrow is to you. If you want to do it, that's great. If you don't, everyone will understand."

"Will people think it's in bad taste if we do?"

He shook his head. "Well, it didn't happen here. The murder, so far as we can tell, took place in the park. So, no, I don't think so. It might even be helpful to us if you open. Though, no pressure or anything."

"How would it help?"

"Well, by now, half the town has already heard about the murder. You know Sweet River. There will be all kinds of folks trying to get a look at the crime scene tomorrow. But your big opening would be a great distraction. And, like you said, this business isn't just yours. Everyone who has a booth in here has been looking forward to it. I say carry on as usual if you're up for it."

I nodded. "I'll think about it tonight."

Jake, the fire chief and owner of the local feed store, poked his head in the back door, and I wiped my face with my hands, hoping that I wasn't as scary looking as I felt. Not that I cared what he thought, of course.

But he was a crazy-handsome man.

"Hey, Ainsley, you doing okay?"

I nodded, not really trusting my voice.

"My guys helped get the area cordoned off for you, Greg, so your people can focus on the crime scene. Is there anything else you need?"

"Could one of you take Ainsley and George home?" my brother asked.

"No. I mean. I'll be fine. You're busy and—" I was blabbering.

"Not a problem. I'll take her home and have Joe follow me in my truck. And I won't take no for an answer, Ainsley," Jake said. "You've been through a shock. Let me do this for you. It'll make me feel better."

I gave him a brief smile and nodded again. Twenty minutes in close quarters with Jake. On top of everything else, well, it was a lot. I'd had a dumb crush on him since I arrived in Sweet River a year ago. He'd been helpful with George, telling me what kind of food to buy and, when George didn't like his bed, special ordering a few for us to try. Jake was also one of my brother's best friends. He had absolutely no interest in me, other than being friends, which was why that crush never went anywhere.

Not that I was really interested.

Keep telling yourself that.

Ten minutes later we were in my SUV, which normally felt large, even with George. But Jake, who was well over six foot four, and built like a linebacker, filled the space on the driver's side.

Nothing like having the short-haired version of Thor driving you home.

And I wasn't the only one slightly taken with Jake. George Clooney had his chin on the poor man's shoulder.

"Do you want to stop at the Dairy Queen and get some dinner?" Jake asked. "I'm betting you haven't eaten in a while."

"I'm not really hungry." Then my stomach growled, making me a liar.

He chuckled, and a few minutes later, he pulled into the drive-thru, which was on the highway, about a half mile from the town square. "Well, we'll grab something, and you can always heat it up later if you don't feel like eating right now. Besides, it's my cheat day."

"Cheat day?"

He shrugged. "We eat kind of crazy at the firehouse, and a lot of the guys have put on weight—like we don't run around with enough pounds of equipment as it is. So, we, the whole station, are following a healthy diet. Tuesdays are usually my day off, so I eat all the bad stuff."

To have a body like his, it probably took a bit of maintenance. Me, well, every day was a cheat day. I always started with good intentions, but usually ended the day with some kind of chocolate. I'd always been curvy, but I was okay with that.

And I really loved food.

A lot.

After ordering some cheeseburgers, fries, and chocolate shakes, he turned to me. "Are you okay to stay on your own tonight? When you were locking up, your brother asked me to tell you that he'd be happier if you stayed at his place."

I scrunched up my face. Greg lived in a small two-bedroom house just a few blocks away from my store. It had the world's tiniest yard. It was basically a back patio with a grill and some chairs where he and his friends hung out. It was a typical bachelor pad. Usually tidy, but sparse. I wanted to be in my house with my things. And poor George was a picky soul. He wouldn't rest well at my brother's.

"I'm good. I'd rather be home in my own bed, and so would George," I said.

"Rurhg," George said from the back seat.

Jake laughed. "I love that Great Danes talk." He reached back and rubbed the dog under his chin. "You're an amazing dog, George."

My dog grunted and then let out a happy sigh.

Lucky dog.

We picked up the burgers at the window, and Jake insisted on paying. "I'm getting Joe's dinner as well," he said, as though that explained why.

"Everyone in town is talking about your art gallery. It's been a while since we've had that sort of excitement in town. I think it's smart of you to open so close to our fall festival. Lots of foot traffic for you."

Handsome and kind. It isn't fair.

"Thanks. How's your mom doing? Greg told me she's interested in making teas? Maybe I should talk to her about selling some in the market."

He chuckled. "Ains. You know I love my mom, but her teas—you might want to try a few before you make that offer. She thinks she's making these magical brews that heal the soul. Her words, not mine. But unless you add about a half cup of sugar or honey, they're kind of hard to drink. If you tell her I said that, I will deny it until my dying breath."

It was sweet he loved his mom so much.

"Duly noted on trying before buying."

"It's good what you're doing. Supporting local artist and craftspeople and bringing the community together. I worry sometimes that we'll turn into one of those ghost towns if we don't keep changing things up."

"Thanks. I just talked to Greg about whether or not to go ahead with everything tomorrow."

He rolled to a stop in front of my house and then turned to me. "Definitely open. It's a good, positive thing you're doing, Ains. The town needs it."

I wish I didn't like the way he said my nickname with that whiskey voice of his.

After dividing up the food, Jake walked me to the door.

George took off around the back of the house. It was his time of night to run around like a crazy dog for all of five minutes, and then he would collapse on his bed or on the end of my sofa for the next twelve hours.

"He looks happy," Jake said.

"That's the great thing about George. One minute he's finding a dead body, the next he's determined to catch a nonexistent squirrel." I opened the door and flipped on the lights inside. I loved this old farmhouse. It had originally belonged to my great-grandmother and was situated on six acres about five miles outside of town. It was quiet.

Tonight, maybe a little too quiet.

"You sure you're going to be all right out here?"

I took the bag of food he held out. "Yep. I've got George; I'm good. Thank you again for running us out here. It's very kind of you."

He waved my comment way. "Ains, I'd do anything for you."

Anything?

Stop it.

He handed me my keys. "Give me your phone."

I frowned. But he held out his hand, so I hadn't misheard him. I had to put the food down on the table by the door and dig through my bag before handing it to him.

He typed something into it and gave it back to me.

"You've got my number. I'm just two pastures over, a lot closer than your brother. If you need anything, you holler, okay?" That soft Texas accent, with his well-worn voice, was just too much. Then he gave me that devastating smile of his, the knee-weakening grin that had me holding on to the door to stay up.

"Thanks. Have a good night." My voice wasn't quivering at all, for which I was most grateful.

After he and Joe left, I put the food on the table and sat down. What a crazy day. My mind was jumping from one thing to another, and I couldn't stop thinking about what happened. Who would commit such a crime? And was the town in danger? I absolutely did not want my friends in town to suffer. I knew Greg would not calm down until the murderer was caught, but I couldn't stop pondering how I could help.

After flipping on the television to my favorite home show, I settled in to eat.

I swear Dairy Queen cheeseburgers are made out of crack. I could eat one every day and not get tired of them.

The events of the day whirled through my brain once again, despite the droning TV, until George's barking got my attention. He seldom did that unless he'd cornered some poor animal. I ran for the back door, threw it open and skidded to a stop.

He was right by the back door, his large body vibrating with fury, barking at the fence as if the zombie apocalypse was nigh.

"George!" He moved in front of me protectively. Then that same sort of growl he'd used at the park came out.

My stomach tightened with dread, and a chill broke out along my skin.

"Is someone there?" I whispered. That was a dumb question, especially since I really, really didn't want an answer.

We were out in the middle of nowhere, and lots of animals roamed the forests behind my property. It had to be a wolf or a coyote. Knowing George, it could be a squirrel.

"Come on, boy. Let's go inside."

Behind locked doors where I'd feel much safer.

He growled again, but he backed into the house with me. After I locked the door, he stood there as a sentry for a good three or four minutes. I grabbed my cell phone, and was about to call my brother, when George stopped. He cocked his head and then went in search of his food and drink bowls.

I breathed a heavy sigh of relief.

My hands shook.

What if I'd seen the murderer and didn't realize it? And worse, what if the murderer had seen me and was out there watching the house? Something really needed to be done about this wandering murderer!

Chapter Three

AFTER SOME EARLY morning calls from Maria, Mrs. Whedon, and a few others with booths at the shop confirming their attendance for the grand opening, I got ready and headed into town. I had been awake most of the night running through potential murder suspects in my head, trying to put together a short list of people for Greg to interview. Anyone and everyone who had ever given me the creeps or the willies.

Needless to say, sleep had not been my friend.

To make room for the customers, I parked in the back, where there were a few spaces for those who owned stores on Main Street. The opening wasn't scheduled for another hour, but as George and I made our way to the front of the store, a long line of people waited to get in.

"Oh. Wow," I said to George. "I guess it's a good thing we're here."

I turned everything on and made sure the computers that we used as registers were ready to roll.

A half hour later, there was a knock on the back door. I'd sent a text asking those manning their booths today to come in from the rear.

Michael was there with a dolly full of wine cases and a package of small paper cups. "Did you see that crowd out front? I told you there was no reason to worry." He smiled, and I opened the door wider so he could get in.

"You were right about the curiosity, I guess. And, Michael, I know he wasn't very nice to you, but I'm sorry that guy you were talking to is dead."

He shook his head. "It's awful, really. Rick was not a great person, but no one deserves to be murdered like that. And I'm even sorrier you had to find him. I mean, he'd just moved here. He couldn't have known that many people. He could get a person riled up, don't get me wrong. But murder? Just doesn't make sense. I don't even remember the last time we had something like that happen in Sweet River."

"Maria told me last night that it had been almost forty years. I have a feeling every time I go out to the park with George, I'm going to remember."

And I'd also be searching for clues as to what happened.

"It's a sad business," Michael said.

As he backed into the building with the dolly, he paused to stare out at the park. The police tape was just visible up on the hill. My shoulders shook, and dread crawled down my spine.

"Well, come on, boy," said Mrs. Whedon, who had walked up. "We need to get in to man our stations, and you're blocking the way."

Michael seemed to check himself and then smiled down at the old woman. "Morning, Mrs. Whedon."

"Morning. Busy day ahead. Don't you have things you should be doing?" She turned that wicked stare on me.

"Yes, ma'am. Since you guys are here, I'll just leave the back door unlocked."

At nine fifty-eight, I announced over the PA system that I was opening the doors. There was a mad dash as people streamed in. While many of them went for the various booths, four women headed straight for the checkout counter. I propped the door open and went to see what they wanted.

They were piling casserole dishes on the counter.

"How are you, dear? Such a terrible thing you suffered yesterday. We wanted to bring you some food, so you didn't have to think about cooking," an older woman with curly white hair said. "If we'd known earlier last night, we would have brought it out to the house."

"Um. Thank you. This is…" Weird. I could see why they might take food to the murdered man's family, but I'd just found him. I didn't deserve their kindness.

"So traumatic," the white-haired woman said. "I'm Helen Irby, and these lovely ladies are all a part of the Widow Circle. We always try to help families out during times of trouble."

"That's very kind of you," I said. "Really."

"So, what can you tell us about the victim? Someone said his head was bashed in. Did you know he and his wife had just moved to town? We're headed to her house next." Helen shot the words at me like bullets from a gun. I had to take a moment to think about what she'd said.

No. I didn't know any of that. I'd assumed, since he was a part of some bigger company trying to buy Michael's place, that he was from out of town. Obviously, if I was going to search for answers on my own to help Greg and the investigation, I needed to know a lot more about Rick, his family and his business.

"I feel so sorry for his family," she said. From the way he treated Shannon and Michael, he couldn't have been a terribly nice man.

"I'm Erma," said the tiny woman next to Helen. "I heard that they already have a suspect in the murder and that there could be an arrest today. My nephew Kevin works as one of the assistant deputies while he goes to college. I'm so proud of that boy. Anyhoo, he was telling me that it's pretty open and shut. They're just waiting for some fingerprints or something."

I shivered again. Funny. I'd called my brother this morning and he hadn't told me a darn thing, just that it was an active investigation and he couldn't discuss it.

Seemed these women had more information than Greg was sharing. Probably a good idea for me to question them after they met with the widow. I might be able to pick up additional information.

"You better get these casseroles in the fridge," said Helen. "We have some shopping to do, ladies, and then we'll visit the new widow. Oh, and let us know when your book club meets. We all want to join," she said.

I handed her the flyer with all of the upcoming classes and events listed. "And come find me when you're on your way out to visit the widow. This is my town now, too, and I want to pay my respects and send a basket of goodies."

Helen winked and the ladies disappeared down an aisle.

My brain hurt. There was no other way to explain it. I asked Maria to help me put the casseroles in the fridge and put together a basket of prepackaged food for the new widow.

Bless Your Art was so crowded that we didn't have time to think most of the day. There'd been a few hiccups but nothing that wasn't easily fixed.

Six hours later, the sales on our first day had far exceeded anything I could have imagined.

The number made no sense.

We'd made our first month's forecast in profits, in one day.

One. Day.

Of course, that probably had to do with the fact that everyone in Sweet River wanted to ask me about what I'd seen and share their theories. When I wasn't able to tell them anything, they went off to shop.

To get out of telling the story a thousand times, we explained that the police had asked me not to say anything. Which meant everyone knew the whole story an hour later and I hadn't said a word.

That's the way small towns worked.

This town was full of gossips, and I was certain every single one of them had been in the store.

We were about to close when three police cars with sirens blaring and lights flashing pulled up in front of the store.

"What's going on?" I asked Samantha, who had arrived after school to help at the register. She'd been a godsend today. Turned out the cheerleading book nerd was also good at math and science. She could tally as fast as the computer scanners we used. And she was just so darn cheerful, I'm sure it helped balance out my silence. While I'd functioned on some level and even managed to smile a few times, I felt like

I was in some kind of *Twilight Zone* episode where my world had shifted on its axis.

I worried I might never feel like myself again.

"Did someone maybe trip an alarm?" Samantha asked. "You've got so much security in this place, it's possible."

My brother came through the door.

"Hey, we were about to close up. What's going on?" I asked.

"I need you to lock the front door and not let anyone else in. Are there any customers still here?"

"No. We just checked out the last of them."

The detective I'd talked to yesterday came through the door. She nodded toward me. "I sent Dickens around the back, just in case he tries to run," she said.

My brother frowned. "I don't think he'll do that. He's a good man."

"Who murdered someone."

"Allegedly murdered. I told you, those fingerprints have a very good reason for being on the bottle," Greg said.

"Who?" I asked. Someone in my store was accused of murder? It didn't make sense. The checkout area was raised so I could see over the whole place. I glanced around to see who was left. Everyone was focused on my brother and the detective.

Then the detective headed to Michael's booth. He watched her walk toward him, and when she started reading his rights, he shook his head.

"No," he said. "I wouldn't hurt anyone."

"You have the right to remain silent," the detective continued. And then when she finished reading his rights, she asked him to put his hands behind his back and cuffed him.

"I don't think that's necessary," Greg said.

"By the book," the detective said. "You want it all by the book. He's a friend of yours—you know we have to do it this way."

"Greg, come on. You can't believe I would do something like this," Michael said, his voice clogged with emotion. It was almost as if he were about to cry. But there was no denying the look on his face—he was shocked. He couldn't believe what they were accusing him of, and there was no way he was that good of an actor. "This isn't real. I— Ainsley, call Shannon. I can't believe this."

"I will," I squeaked. I'd known him since the first week I arrived in Sweet River. I'd spent a lot of time with him and Shannon. He was fond of dogs and kittens and volunteered at the retirement home two nights a week, even though his winery was a booming business.

He wasn't someone who could commit murder. He rescued puppies and worked the suicide hotline. He brought me coffee and helped me renovate Bless Your Art. Michael wouldn't hurt a fly. He lived to help people and give back to his community.

"I'm going to lock the door," Samantha said beside me. "Maybe you should go ahead and call his fiancée. Ainsley, are you okay?"

"What? Oh. Um. Thanks." I picked up my cell phone.

Shannon started speaking as soon as she answered. "How was the first day?" She sounded so chipper, I couldn't take it. "I texted Michael a bit ago, and he said it was crazy with everything that happened."

"Shannon." It came out as a croak and maybe half a sob. This day was definitely getting to me.

"Are you okay?"

"It's Michael," I said finally. "He's—"

"What?" she cried. "Did something happen to him? Where is he?"

"Arrested. Michael was arrested for the murder of the man in the park."

Chapter Four

A FEW MINUTES later, I stared out the window of the store as the last of the police cars pulled away. Shannon was sobbing on the other end of the line. I let her cry because I wasn't sure what else to do. Eventually, the crying turned to a whimper.

"Ainsley," she said, "please talk to your brother. He'll listen to you. Find out what's going on for me."

I was the last person my brother would listen to given his need to be impartial and unbiased on this case, but I wasn't telling her that. "Absolutely. You just hang tight. Well, maybe find him a lawyer." We hung up.

When I turned around to the front counter, I found the vendors had circled around and stared at me expectantly.

"She didn't take the news well," I said, not sure what they wanted me to say.

"Of course, she didn't," Maria said.

"Someone should make certain she's all right," said Mrs. Whedon. "Shannon shouldn't be alone. And we need to let Michael's family know. They're going to be devastated. He shows up every Sunday morning like clockwork to make them breakfast."

"I'll help with Shannon. My husband has the kids for at least another hour," Maria said.

"I'll call his parents," Pete, who ran a booth with medieval items he made for Renaissance fairs and people who were fond of the time period, said. "I go to church with them. And I sometimes play poker with his dad Cliff on Friday nights."

"We'll go with Maria and check on Shannon. We'll take her some of the food people brought in today," Cari said. She and her son had a booth that carried all of Cari's jams, and just about anything that could be pickled.

"The rest of us will sweep up and get things ready for tomorrow," Don said. He had a booth with wooden animals he carved. "Ainsley, you need to go talk some sense into your brother. You know Rick had a lot of enemies and Michael wasn't one of them."

"So, none of you believe he did it, either?" Okay, it wasn't my brightest moment, but they seemed as certain of Michael's innocence as me. And they had all known Michael since he was born.

"No," they said in unison.

I smiled, a real one for the first time since I'd seen the body. "Cari, you have the other set of keys. Can you give those to Don? I'm going to the station. You guys are right. Obviously, they have all of this terribly wrong. Don you'll be all right?"

"Don't worry. I'll lock up and turn off the lights," he said. He looked like Santa Claus and had the disposition of the jolly old elf, which was why many of the children in town were always very good around him.

I was about to step out the door, when there was a strange sound from behind the counter. "Oh. George. Um, I guess you're coming with me." He stood up as if he understood exactly what I'd said.

I didn't trust myself to drive, and it was only two blocks to the station. George needed a stretch and—to be honest—I didn't know what I was going to say when I got there. I needed some time to clear my head. My brother would be angry if I tried to meddle, but he needed to know the additional information about Rick and other possible motives. I walked the two blocks and went around the back of the courthouse where the police station was.

When I opened the door, the place was busier than I'd ever seen it. The officers bustled in and out of offices. It reminded me of a scene from *Alice in Wonderland* with the White Rabbit running around. Nothing ever happened in this town. Most of the time the people working here were playing solitaire or poker on their computers.

"Evening, Ainsley. How are you?" Kevin, who was working the front desk, asked. I had a feeling he was the Kevin Erma had mentioned earlier today. "Do you need to talk to the sheriff?"

"Yes," I said. "Is it okay for me to go back?"

Kevin shook his head. "He's got someone in the office right now. They're doing an interview. You'll have to wait until he's done, or I can give him a message."

"I'll wait. Who is he with?" I leaned my head to the right, but the blinds were closed in Greg's office.

"Dooley's in there right now. But it's been one right after another all day," Kevin said. "It's not looking good for Michael."

Kevin was one of the guys on Michael's flag football

team, along with my brother, Jake, Kane, who was the local coroner, and a couple of other guys from the station.

"They have the wrong man," I said. George grunted beside me.

Kevin shrugged. "Sometimes people do things they don't mean to. Sometimes they do it on purpose. But like I said, it's not looking good."

"Even you're turning against him?"

Michael had been friends with these guys. How could they turn on him so quickly? And weren't people supposed to be innocent until proven guilty?

"Can't talk about the case but the evidence is there." The phone rang. "I don't know how long he'll be, but you can wait on the bench over there." Kevin pointed to the small lobby area.

I sat down with George and tried to gather my thoughts. But my mind wouldn't settle. Flashes of the day whirled through my head like a tornado on a path of destruction. Maybe I was still in shock.

I went over the facts. There was no way Michael killed anyone. Sure, a wine bottle had been involved, but Michael was a winemaker, so his fingerprints could definitely be on many bottles all over town. I needed to find out what they thought the motive was. If the police were going to railroad a perfectly innocent man, someone had to be looking out for him and bring in the right suspect.

I was so lost in my thoughts that it took me a minute to realize someone was talking to me.

"You okay, Ains?"

I glanced up to find my brother staring down at me.

Dooley, who owned one of the diners on the town square, waved as he walked past, and I waved back. I wonder what he'd said to my brother.

"Uh. Yes."

"Did you have something you wanted to add to your statement?"

"My statement? No. I wanted to check on Michael. Have you let him go yet? Did you get it sorted?"

He sighed and rubbed the bridge of his nose with his fingertips. "It doesn't work like that, Ainsley. He had motive and opportunity, and we have evidence that puts him at the scene."

"But."

"Miss McGregor." Lucy the detective from the day before came up to stand next to my brother. "You were working early yesterday at your shop, correct?"

"Yes," I said wondering what that had to do with anything.

"Did you see Mr. Caldwell arguing with the victim?"

Oh. No. Why did I come here? I couldn't lie but no way was I telling them exactly what I'd seen. "Um." I pursed my lips. "I saw a lot of people that day. He could have been."

That was the truth at least.

"The sheriff tells me you have a good memory when it comes to events and things. Are you sure you didn't hear what they were discussing?" Lucy crossed her arms and gave me that look like she knew I was evading her question.

"I was more interested in getting my store ready to open," I said.

That was also true.

"Could you answer the question directly please?"

The room was quiet, and everyone stared at me. There was no way I'd ever contribute to Michael's troubles and the truth about what I heard and saw might do exactly that. I'd tell my brother soon, but for right now I was done.

"If this is official, shouldn't we be in a room where there aren't so many ears? It's no wonder half the town seems to know more about this than you do." I waved a hand toward her and my brother.

Maybe it was mean, but I needed a distraction. I was most definitely going to evade her questions for as long as possible. "I'm not sure I appreciate how you're conducting this investigation. I'd hate to have to file a formal complaint, Detective, because you fail to have the common decency to do this sort of thing privately. But it doesn't matter. I didn't come down here to be questioned. I'm tired. I wanted to make sure my friend was all right. End of story. If you want to talk to me again, you know where I live."

I gave my brother a harsh look. How dare he let her ambush me like that. "And you—" I pointed at him "—should be ashamed of yourself."

I was going to regret that later, but I didn't care. I couldn't believe how quickly these people had turned against their friend.

"Come on, George." He followed me out of the station.

Maybe my brother wouldn't listen to reason but there was no way I would allow an innocent man to go to prison.

And I would not allow some detective who was trying to prove herself help send him there. First, I had to talk to the diner owner, Dooley. Whatever he'd told the police had helped put poor Michael in a cell.

I pulled my phone out of my pocket. "Hey, Dooley, I need a to-go order."

A few minutes later, I waited at the takeout window that faced Main Street. To my right was the door where patrons could go in to eat at the fifties-style diner with its red and white leather seats and Formica tables. He was known for some of the best burgers and fried chicken in Texas.

If it were a couple of hours earlier, there might be a line around the block of people waiting for either the window or to go inside.

"Hey, Red, what's up?" Dooley asked as he slid the window open.

"Hi, I'm surprised you're working the window." I figured I'd have to ask for him, as he was usually in the back managing the busy kitchen.

He shrugged. "It's late, so we're slow. I sent some of the staff home when I got back. Your order should be up in a few." He started to slide the window back.

I waved a hand. "I—uh, is there any chance you could tell me what the police were asking you? Was it about Michael? And before you call me nosy and tell me to butt out, I promised Shannon I'd find out whatever I could and my brother is being a—well, not so forthcoming."

He was a big man, round and arms the size of fire hydrants. He told me once his friends called him Dooley because he was built like one of those giant trucks and he was kind of loud, even when trying to whisper. He smirked and then nodded. "I fcel sorry for Shannon and Michael. I don't think he did this, but they seem convinced."

"So, what did you tell them?"

"They wanted to know about an argument that happened in the diner last night. Michael had met the guy for dinner. They'd been talking business and things got a bit heated. I came out from the back and told them to calm down. Michael apologized but the other guy stood up like he was going to punch me or something. Made some not-so-nice comments about my food. Then he told Michael he'd be sorry. No way he'd survive without him. Then he left."

Weird. What did all of that mean?

"What did Michael do after that?"

"He just sat there for a few minutes and then left cash on table for his bill."

I had no idea when the murder had occurred, but the timeline didn't sound so great for my friend. If they argued and he followed him out, that couldn't be good.

After picking up the food, I headed over to Shannon's apartment above the coffee shop. She had the second floor for her living space, and a rooftop terrace. That's where I found her curled up in one of her lawn chairs with a glass of wine.

Her face blotchy from crying, she sat up straighter when George and I made it up the stairs. "I thought Maria or someone would be here with you," I said.

She shook her head. "I sent them all home. I can't believe this, Ainsley. Tell me you found something out."

I pursed my lips.

"That bad?" She sighed. "You know he had nothing to do with this, right?"

"I do. No matter how mad someone might make him, he

would never hurt anyone. Dooley told me that Michael and the victim had dinner at Dooley's last night. Were they doing business?"

She took her long hair out of the messy ponytail and then redid it. "They were talking about it. This is just so messed up." She started to cry again. George put his head in her lap, which made her smile a bit.

"It's going to be okay." I mean, I really hoped so. But, like she said, things were definitely messed up. I scooted next to her on the big wooden chair and wrapped my arms around her.

"They wouldn't let me see him," she said. "I tried. They said there is a bail hearing in the morning. I talked to the bail bondsmen. I can put my store up for collateral."

I squeezed her tight. "Let's hope it doesn't come to that. Help me sort this out so I can go to my brother with facts. Where were you last night? You two are usually joined at the hip."

"Oh, Ains, if only I'd been where I was supposed to be none of this would have happened." She pulled away and reached for a tissue. "I was supposed to be at that dinner at Dooley's. But—"

"What?" I turned to face her.

"That slime ball, and yes I know it's awful to speak ill of the dead, made a pass at me."

"That's awful. What did you do?"

"I yelled at him. He's married. I mean, what a creeper. And hello?" She pointed to her ring. "Newly engaged. He was not a nice person and Michael figured that out about ten minutes into their first conversation. They'd been emailing for months about Rick's company helping Michael to expand his wine. They'd promised national distribution for him.

"I feel so bad because Michael was so excited—until they met face-to-face. He knew, instantly, that this guy was not above board. But he couldn't get rid of him. As in, actually told him at least three times he was no longer interested but the guy wouldn't back off.

"After I told him what he could do with his so-called plan and I wondered what his wife might think about his asking me out, he left. Well, you saw him at the coffee shop. Creeper. Did I say that already?"

"Can't say I disagree. Did Michael know that he hit on you?"

She wrung her hands together. "I didn't say anything to him. It would just upset him, and he was already so stressed."

Well, that would have made for good motive, though. I was serious when I promised her that I knew there was no way Michael had killed anyone. Maybe punched the guy in the face, but murder—no way.

"Is the winery okay?"

She blew out a big breath. "Yes and no. It's solvent but just barely. He expanded a bit too quickly and lately there's been one big expense after another. That's why he'd been reaching out to see if someone wanted to invest a little or help get the wine some national visibility. There were quite a few people interested but after all this insanity they're probably running for the hills. Michael is a wonderful guy and this winery is everything to him. It will crush him if it goes under."

Killing someone definitely wouldn't be good for business. "Well, we just need a plan."

Shannon raised her eyes to the heavens. "Ainsley, not everything is about having plans. This isn't your business where you have to figure out all contingencies. We just need to get your brother to have a bit of common sense. He's known Michael for as long as he's lived here, he knows he didn't do it."

"You're under a lot of stress, so I'm going to ignore your dig about me making plans. But that's exactly what we need. First, and you and I have watched enough detective shows to understand this, we need to find out who else might have wanted Rick dead, right?"

She nodded.

"The police feel like they have solid evidence against Michael. So, we have to show them they're wrong."

George seemed to grunt in agreement.

"You're a very good friend," Shannon said and then sniffled again.

"I am, which is why I brought that Cuban sandwich you like so much from Dooley's."

"Oh, Ains, I don't know if I can eat."

Some people couldn't eat when stressed; I'm the opposite. "And some bourbon pecan pie."

Shannon gave me a weak smile. "Oh. That maybe I could eat. It's like you know me."

I did—better than just about everyone in town, except for her brother. That's why I was going to do everything in my power to find out what happened to Rick.

And the first place I was going to start was at the hearing bright and early in the morning.

Chapter Five

AFTER MAKING SURE everything was ready at the shop, and with a promise from Maria that she'd watch the register and George Clooney, I headed to the courthouse.

But the hearing was over, and Shannon was in the hallway with several friends and guys in suits.

"What happened?" I glanced down at my watch. "I thought it was at eight thirty?" It was only a quarter past the hour.

Shannon swallowed hard. "They were running early—I barely made it here. And the bail is set at a quarter of a million."

Yikes. Even if she put her shop up, it wouldn't be enough collateral.

"What can I do to help? We could do a fund-raiser or something."

She took my arm and pulled me to the side, away from everyone. "I had a chance to talk to him. He doesn't want me to risk my business. It's only a risk if he runs away and I know he's not going to do that. But it's weird. He says he's okay in the county lockup. That it's not that bad."

"That's so wrong in a hundred different ways," I said. "It sounds like he's trying to be brave. He's not a flight risk, and that seems like a lot. What did the lawyer say? Maybe we should get a better one?"

Shannon shook her head. "Michael's dad sent him. He's some big fancy criminal lawyer. His father offered to put up the bail, but Michael's not going for it. He's not happy about the lawyer but there isn't anyone better. It's so weird. It's like he feels he deserves to be in jail." Shannon pushed her long hair off her face. "Can you try to talk some sense into him? Meanwhile, I'm going to talk to the bail bondsman and see what I can do. The idea of him spending one more night in there—I just can't take it."

I didn't know Michael didn't get along with his father. My brother had trouble with our dad, as well. Never felt like he was good enough. Dad hadn't been happy when neither of us went into the family business of making furniture, but my brother probably did get the worst of that.

The last thing our father wanted was for Greg to be a cop. Too dangerous. Making furniture was safe, certain and prone to, well, less death.

"I don't know if they'll let me see him since I'm not his lawyer or his fiancée."

"I put you on his list of visitors. He was allowed five in addition to his lawyer and me. See what you can find out from that brother of yours. I'm willing to risk my coffee shop or do whatever it takes to prove his innocence. People listen to you, Ainsley—please. They trust you and look up to you."

I hugged her. "I'm here for you," I said. "But I'm not a detective and I'm not sure what I can do."

"Just talk to him, please. If nothing else, convince him to take the offer for the bail or let me do it. I may do it without his permission anyway."

It's very hard to tell Shannon no when she really wants something. "Okay." Everything I knew about posting bail came from reading the Stephanie Plum books by Janet Evanovich. But I'd promised my friend I'd try, so I headed out to see if I could talk to Michael.

Twenty minutes later, I was escorted into a blah, grayish-green room that had two tables and some chairs at the police station. I expected Michael to show up in a jumpsuit and handcuffs, but he wore jeans and a clean blue button-down. His hair was neatly combed but he had dark circles under his eyes like he hadn't slept for years.

"Ainsley?" He obviously hadn't been expecting me.

"Hey, how are you? I mean, given the circumstances." *Dumb question, Ainsley.*

He shrugged as he sat down across from me. "Did Shannon send you?"

"I actually came by last night, but they wouldn't let me see you." Okay, that wasn't exactly true. I'd stormed out to avoid questions, but I had originally come to check on Michael.

"Oh. Thanks. Is Shannon okay? She kept it together at the courthouse, but I could tell she'd been crying. I feel so bad for her—this has to be so embarrassing. Man, that she's been drawn into all this crazy is just killing me."

"Then why won't you take the offer to pay for your bail?"

He crossed his arms and leaned back in the metal chair. "If I let my parents help me out, it comes with strings. Shannon doesn't get that. She hasn't met them yet, and there's a reason for that. I don't want them to taint my relationship with her. And no way I'm letting her put the shop up as collateral.

"I keep hoping your brother will find something that gets me out of here. It's nuts that they even think I'm a suspect. Did you know he was killed with a wine bottle? One of mine? How dumb would I have to be to use that as a weapon, and of course it has my fingerprints all over it."

I pursed my lips. It didn't make sense. Sure, that detective might be out to make her career, but my brother was brilliant. I'd never tell him that, of course.

"Run me through what happened, after you left Dooley's. He says hello, by the way."

Michael smiled. It didn't reach his eyes, though.

"Dooley's a good guy. I had dinner with Rick. The guy—I'm not going to lie. He's a jerk. In the emails he'd been so positive and had even given me some creative ideas about temporary fixes to help the winery out. He and his wife had moved to Gruene. He's been helping to launch some of the new wineries there.

"I should have known he was too good to be true. As soon as I met him face-to-face, there was a smarmy evilness to him. Never got such a bad vibe off of someone so fast. Do you know what I mean? Like you can see he's evil to the core?"

I nodded.

"I thanked him for coming out to the winery, but said that I'd decided to go a different way, which in my head, was any way that didn't include him or the company he worked for. He was mad. Cussed me out right then and again at Bless Your Art. But later he texted and asked that I meet him at Dooley's for dinner. Said he wanted to part on good terms.

"I should have said, no. But I went to the dinner. Everything was fine until we started talking about the business again. He lost his temper and created a scene in front of everyone. But it wasn't just me he was mad at. I could tell he was agitated about something else—he was just taking his temper out on me. I was about to get up and leave, when he screamed some obscenities and left."

I leaned my elbows on the table. "Were you mad?"

Shaking his head, he turned to look out the only window in the room. Everyone in the police station was staring at him, and then they all turned away quickly pretending to work.

Michael rubbed his temple with his hand. "More embarrassed than anything," he said. "I finished my food—you know I'm not leaving Dooley's food on the table no matter what happened. Anyway, about five minutes later I went home. I remember thinking it was weird the light was on in the barn. We try to keep things pretty green, and don't waste electricity. I didn't remember leaving it on but maybe I did. I'd been counting cases right before I left for the dinner. We had about a hundred headed to a party in Austin. But I was there alone all night."

I believed him and there was no way it was just the wine bottle that had him behind bars. The police had to have a lot more than that. Even I knew that was circumstantial. I needed to talk to my brother.

"Is there anything I can get for you? Anything you need?"

"Nah. Just look after the booth? Ask Don if he can open up the samples. Oh, and keep an eye on the teens who come in. I caught a few that first day trying to scam some free samples of the wine from me."

I stood up. As I did, one of the officers opened the door. "You take care, Michael. Don't worry. We'll get this sorted."

He and the officer headed down the long hallway. "Thanks," he said.

I wasn't sure what to do next, but I had to talk to my brother. The murder weapon was way too obvious. Easily traceable. I needed to figure out where the bottle had been lifted—the winery, the booth, or from Michael's house? Because it should be so easy to trace, Greg definitely had to have something else to arrest and charge Michael with.

Without asking for permission, I headed to my brother's office. It was locked and even with the blinds pulled, I could see the light was off. Just as well, as I needed to get to the shop.

I'd just stepped outside of the station when I heard the blood-curdling scream.

Running around to the side of the courthouse I found two women yelling at one another. One was tall with dark hair in a bun. She wore a green dress that was straight out of the Jackie O era. The other one was much younger in tight jeans and a rock band T-shirt. But it was hard to see their features as they circled one another in a threatening way.

I was about to run back to the station to grab someone, when my brother came jogging around the corner with several cups of coffee in one of those containers that hold multiple. I was surprised Shannon had served him. He put the coffee on the edge of the stone ledge leading down to the basement where the coroner's office and the morgue were.

"Stop!" He gave them his best I'm Mr. Officer of the Law and you better shut it voice.

They paused, as did I. Never in my life had I heard him sound so scary. The door down to the basement opened and shut. Idris Elba walked out. Okay, so Kane is not Idris Elba, but they could be twins. He's the coroner and I've been at some of the barbeques my brother throws with him, and Jake. They're my brother's best friends, and they're a handsome lot. If a girl was interested in that sort of thing.

Me, not so much. At least, not yet. I still wasn't over my last disastrous relationship. Eddy, my giraffe tattoo, was a visual reminder of what happened when I stuck my neck out for people—so it was doubly crazy that I was running around town trying to solve Rick's murder and free Michael.

"I told them to take it outside," Kane said. "I had no idea it would escalate like this."

"You," my brother ordered pointing to the younger of the two women, "stand over there." She moved a few feet in front of me on the sidewalk. "You," he ordered the older one, "stand by Kane. And then tell me what this is about."

"I came to identify the body," the woman said. "I'm Rachel Dean and Rick is—I mean, was my husband."

"At least, that's what she keeps saying," said the younger woman. "I'm Caroline Dean, and I'm his wife. She's lying. I don't know why."

Ohhhh. I was starting to get the picture and I had a feeling this story was about to get way more interesting. A crowd started to gather on the street, and my brother's eyebrows drew together. "Kane, will you help me escort these two women to my office?"

The women started to protest but he held up a hand. "One more word, and grieving widows or not, I'll arrest you for disturbing the peace." That seemed to mollify them. They followed Kane around the corner.

I was about to follow. This was most certainly an interesting development in the case.

"Ainsley, what are you doing here?" my brother asked as he picked up the container with the coffee.

"I was talking to Michael. I can't believe that guy was married to two women at the same time. Surely that's more motive than anything Michael might have."

His brows drew even deeper together. "There's a line of people waiting outside your store. Maybe you should mind your business, and let the police handle the case."

I was about to protest but I knew that look.

"You don't have to be so rude," I said through gritted teeth.

His eyebrow went up.

Whatever. There'd be no talking to him right now. Besides, he had his hands busy with those widows. But even if I had to show up at his house with a lasagna, made from our mother's recipe, he was going to talk to me. Actually, that wasn't such a bad idea.

I turned the corner to find that he hadn't lied. There was a line of at least thirty people waiting to get inside. I backtracked and went around the park side of the building on Main Street, so I could go in the back entrance.

Every time I walked into my store, a sense of pride

welled within me. It was so much more than I'd ever dreamed. Even with all the crazy, the sense that I'd done the right thing going after my dreams was there.

As I made my way through the booths, Mrs. Whedon called out, "What did you find out? We can do one of those kickstand things to raise money if we need to—or a bake sale." Pretty sure she meant kickstarter but no way was I telling her. Today the older woman wore her signature green, but in a caftan studded with diamonds, along with some very sensible sneakers in her favorite color.

Everyone who was in the store gathered around. I explained what happened and why he didn't want the bail quite yet. Then I told them about the two women and the disaster on the sidewalk.

"Well, just goes to show that guy wasn't the best," Don said. "Seems to me those women have more reason to kill him than anyone else."

"I agree. But they arrested Michael because of the evidence, more than just the wine bottle."

"What did you find out from your brother?" Maria asked.

"Nothing. He was busy with those women. But I'm going to try and talk to him later."

"We should do a murder board like on *Death in Paradise*," Maria said. "I think I may have an old one out in my garage that the kids used."

We all stared at her blankly.

"What?" she asked.

"What is *Death in Paradise*?" Mrs. Whedon asked.

"It's a British mystery show set on a Caribbean island,"

Maria said. "I'd live there if it wasn't a fake island, I didn't have five kids and it wasn't filled with super sophisticated murderers. Like, every episode is some elaborate murder. Anyway, at the police station, they have a whiteboard where they put up the pictures and clues they find. We could do that. Set it up in the break room or one of the classrooms upstairs. And then if one of us hears something we can write it down."

It wasn't a bad idea and might help me keep things straight in my head.

"I agree," I said, "with one condition. That we keep all of this to ourselves. If my brother got wind of us trying to help—well, I'd rather not find out what he'd do. So, this is just between us, right?"

Everyone agreed.

Of course, I shouldn't have been surprised when two hours later, Ms. Helen and her troop of women showed up demanding to see the murder board.

I sighed. "I don't know what you're talking about," I said. So much for secrets in this place.

"Erma overheard Don and Mrs. Whedon talking about who they were going to put on the murder board as suspects. We have some ideas of our own. There's no use trying to pretend you don't know what we're talking about. I'm telling you, we can help." She glanced around to see if anyone was listening, and then lowered her voice. "Let's discuss it tonight at the book club."

Oh, heck. I'd forgotten about the book club. So much for using lasagna to pry secrets from my brother tonight.

"Okay but let's keep it quiet. I'll tell you what I told the others. If my brother finds out, I'll be in big trouble. We all will."

This was going to go all kinds of wrong. I could feel it.

Chapter Six

EIGHT HOURS LATER we were readying the main conference room in the back of the store for the book club
meeting. Maria brought two big whiteboards that we sat up
on easels.

The Hens, that's what Erma and Helen liked to call
themselves, had arrived with a list of suspects an arm long,
and two different types of casseroles. Don brought some
desserts his wife, Peggy, had made. One was a cake in the
shape of a butterfly; the other was a cheesecake with white
chocolate sauce that I kind of wanted to take home and eat
the whole thing by myself.

I had no idea how stressful it would be talking about
murder. We'd whittled down the suspects to about three,
and each of them seemed to have more reason to kill the
poor victim than Michael did.

"When we went to the wife's house, she was one cold
fish," said Helen. "She was not happy about her, and I
quote, 'Lying, cheating, scumbag of a husband, having
something on the side.' As far as she's concerned, he got
what he deserved. Though, I heard when she was talking to
the police that she had crocodile tears. I tell you, she did it."

Erma nodded.

I'd erased a few of the other names we'd taken off the

list, including my friend Shannon. Someone else had seen them arguing at the coffee shop. But there was no way she could do it. She's a tiny thing and it takes a lot of force to kill someone with a wine bottle. At least, that's what Don had found out from the coroner, Kane. I had plans to chat with him the next day.

"Oh, and that mistress." Erma shook her head as she spoke. "That young woman needs to learn some manners. Didn't even want to take the rolls and roast beef we brought her. Told us she was in mourning, that she didn't know us, and then asked us to leave. So rude. Who turns away free food? Guilty people, that's who. Probably eating her up inside."

I had to bite back a smile. But wrote the mistress on the whiteboard. And was she a mistress if she thought she was married to Rick? I had to find out what all that was about.

"There's also a new guy snooping around Michael's winery," Mrs. Whedon said. "Says he's a friend and there to help with the harvest. Danny something. Shannon said he was a good guy."

I wondered why she'd been out at the winery, but she did like a good Chardonnay, so who was I to judge? I wrote Danny Something on the board. I'd ask Shannon about him later, or better yet, maybe it was time I drove out to the winery to have a look for myself.

"So, all of them have motive," I said. "Well, except for him." I pointed to the guy helping Shannon. "We'll need to find out why he showed up out of the blue. I don't disagree that seems a bit suspicious."

"Oh, I remember something the wife said," Erma added.

"They had a vacation planned, and she wanted Kane to release the body so they could get him buried and done with. She was still going to some place called the Maldives. I looked it up on Helen's phone. It's a pretty place but she doesn't seem like the world traveler type. I'd be surprised if she'd ever been out of the States."

"I agree," Helen said. "Not the sharpest tool in the shed and neither was that mistress. Maybe that's how he got away with the affair. The wife didn't seem like she had any inkling about anything until all this happened. But the Maldives? Just seems a whole lot of fishy to me."

Hmmmm. That did seem a bit much. No one could blame her for being angry but why the rush on burying the body?

"Don, look up countries that don't have extradition treaties with the U.S. and I wonder if there's a way to find out when that trip was booked."

A few seconds later, Don pulled up a website and showed us all. The Maldives did not have an extradition treaty with the United States.

"You should share all this with the sheriff," Mrs. Whedon said. "It might be enough to get Michael out of jail."

I shrugged. "I will talk to him—I'd already planned to about some other things. Unfortunately, everything we have right now is circumstantial. We need proof. If we can show him that the wife booked the trip after the murder, that might help. Right now, I'd say she or the girlfriend are the best suspects. Now, how about we move on to choosing our book to read this month since that's the real reason we're here?"

There were some chuckles. "Okay," I said, "one of the reasons."

An hour later, we had picked out the book. I took the whiteboards to my office and locked them up. It wouldn't do for anyone outside the group to see our little experiment. The hardest part would be trying to talk to my brother about it. He'd be mad if he discovered we'd been snooping. But they were busy at the station and maybe our little chat could provide some helpful background for him.

I sent him a text.

I'm making dinner tomorrow. Be here at seven.

I walked down the empty aisle to Michael's booth and looked at the wine racks loaded with bottles of wine. Several slots were empty and I noted what kind of wines were in those missing bottles. Maybe one would match up with the murder weapon? Once I noted all the varieties of the missing wine bottles, I went back up to the register to compare sales receipts.

This effort took longer than I thought as Michael had sold way more wine than I had anticipated. There were three bottles unaccounted for: a Chardonnay, a pinot grigio and a rosé.

What had happened to those three bottles? And was the murder weapon among them? I needed to find out more about the bottle used to kill Rick.

I loaded George Clooney in the car and was about to turn on the ignition when my phone dinged.

Kane and Jake want to know if you're making lasagna?

He must have been playing poker with them. Getting

them all to the house would mean I could ask questions without him getting too suspicious. And I might also be able to say things like, "I overheard Helen and Erma talking about the wife and her trip to the Maldives that she's insisting she's still going." Oh, and I had so many questions for Kane after what Don said about the force it would take to kill someone like that. And how tall they might have to be.

Yes. I texted him back.

All I had to do was work a full day, go to the grocery store, come up with a plan to interrogate my brother and his friends, and make a decent lasagna.

George nudged my shoulder.

"I know. I know. You're ready to run around like a maniac. Let's get you home."

I'd have to add making a wine run to my list. Perhaps Danny could help me determine if any bottles were missing from the winery itself.

THE NEXT AFTERNOON, Don promised to lock up the store for me so I could get home and start the lasagna. I'd made the sauce early in the morning and left it in the Crock-Pot to simmer all day.

Since I had to drive past the winery to get home, I decided to stop and get a few bottles to restock. I was about to turn right at the fork in the road on Michael's property when I saw Shannon sitting on the porch with her knees pulled up, and her face in her hands as if she were crying. My insides twisted into a knot. I couldn't imagine what she must be going through. There was a blond guy sitting next to her, who I didn't recognize. He'd better not have been the one to make her cry.

I turned the car to the left up the private drive and pulled up to Michael's farmhouse. It had the same kind of ornate trim mine did but was painted a deep blue with cream-colored trim. Instead of a big red barn like most of the properties around here had, Michael's was painted blue with the logo of his wine on the front. He kept everything neat and tidy.

Shannon lifted her head. Her tear-stained face was my undoing. I breathed deep and then opened the door. After letting George out, I headed her way. My dog seemed to understand the seriousness of the situation and didn't run around like his normal crazy self when he was outside without a leash.

"Hey, what's wrong?"

I pulled a tissue out of my pocket and handed it to her. She dabbed at her nose. "I'm not sure I've ever cried so much as I have the last few days," she said. "Everything was going so well, and now it's all upside down."

"It will get sorted. We all know Michael is innocent."

She nodded.

"I should get back to the vines. I'll let you two chat," the man beside her said as he stood up. "And she's right, Michael will be fine."

"Oh, you don't have to go," Shannon said. "This is my best friend Ainsley. And, Ains, this is Danny. He's been helping with the winery while Michael is a—" That last part came out as a whisper.

I stuck out my hand. He shook it. "It's nice to meet you. But I really should be getting back to help out. They're right in the middle of pruning and it's key that it's done right." He walked off.

I sat down beside my friend, and George stretched out in the grass to our right.

"What happened?"

She just stared out into the yard for the longest time. "He didn't do it, Ainsley."

"I know that," I said. "I have absolutely one hundred percent no doubts about it. We just have to find a way to prove it."

"His lawyer says it isn't looking good. Even though the evidence is circumstantial, and that it makes no sense he would use his own product to kill someone, the police seem to think they've found their man. I don't know what to do. And then I came over to check on things and found something that broke my heart."

"What?" Did she find something in the house?

She stood up and motioned for me to follow her.

Danny was in the vineyards helping to prune the vines, like he said. It appeared he knew what he was talking about. But I had no way of knowing. I hoped he wasn't taking advantage of Shannon.

"Who is that guy?"

Shannon cleared her throat. "Danny? He and Michael have known each other for a long time. They used to work for a big liquor company before Michael opened this place. Danny's company was also interested in investing but with all this…craziness, I doubt anyone will want to touch the place."

I wasn't sure how to ask her what I really wanted to know. "Are you sure he's—uh?" Clever girl. I just couldn't figure out a way to ask her if he was on the up and up.

"He's a good guy. I'm not sure what we'd do around here without him. Like he said, everything has to be pruned before winter gets here. In other parts of the world they do it in February or March, but Michael's a wine genius. He figured out the best time was before winter here in Texas. Even though ours are pretty mild, one freeze and the vines can be ruined if we don't protect them now."

"So, what is it, besides the obvious, that has you so upset?"

She put her arm in mine and guided me to the far side of the barn.

I gasped, and George, who had been trotting along behind us, barked.

There on the side of the barn in big white spray-painted letters was the word: MURDERER.

"When did it happen?"

"I don't know. Danny called me this afternoon when I was closing up. He said I needed to come out so he could show me something. I guess he didn't want to upset me. But he found it first thing this morning. Someone must have been out here last night."

It was cruel. I couldn't imagine anyone in town would do something like this. One of the things I loved about Sweet River was that people were generally quite kind. It was a college town so sure there was some vandalism or craziness every once in a while, but this was just cruel.

"Did you call my brother?"

She pursed her lips. "Like he'd care."

Crud. I'd walked right into that. "He does care. I know it may seem unfair but he's just doing his job. And because Michael is his friend, he has to do it by the book. It's hard to understand. I mean, even I don't get it sometimes. But he's taking absolutely no joy in any of this." I'd seen the strain on his face when those two women were fighting and every time Michael's name came up, he sort of winced.

While I didn't like it any more than Shannon, he was doing his best. Of that, I was certain. My brother came across as kind of laid-back and easygoing, but he was smart and thoughtful. He'd figure this out.

"Ainsley, I know I'm asking a lot, but will you help me?"

"Yes. Anything you need," I said.

"Thank you. I heard about your murder board. Promise me that you'll find who killed that poor man. It wasn't my Michael. And I need him out of that place as soon as possible."

Did everyone in town know about the dumb murder board? My brother would kill me if he found out. I wanted to say I wasn't a detective or that I had no idea how to catch a murderer, but I didn't. I'd help her any way I could. I was a good listener and observer. Maybe I could give my brother the information the book club had picked up and it'd make a difference.

"I'm going to do everything I can to make that happen," I promised. Then I hugged my friend. I squeezed my eyes tightly shut to keep from crying but when I opened them, I found Danny watching carefully under the brim of his ball cap.

I wasn't so sure about that guy. Everything about him showing up, friend or not, was a bit too convenient.

"What's your friend Danny's last name?"

"Avery. Why?"

I squeezed her tight and let go. "Just seems familiar. Maybe I saw him in the store or something. Thought I might know him." That was a bold-faced lie. I was just curious.

"I don't think so," she said. "He's been staying in Michael's house and helping out here since the night Michael was arrested."

What? "Did you call him? How did he find out if he doesn't live here?"

She frowned. "He's a friend, Ains. But I don't know. I assumed one of the workers called him. Michael has an emergency contact list in the winery office. I'm pretty sure Danny is at the top of the list. He's been around a lot the last few years and really is a good friend."

I smiled. "You've met me, I'm pretty much suspicious of everyone. I'm sure he's a great guy." Still it might be worth checking Mr. Avery out. Even though I should have been grateful that he was there to keep things running for my friend.

George barked. And I remembered why I'd come. "Hey, I'm having my brother and his friends over for some lasagna. Would you like to come?"

"No thanks. I mean, think about it, Ainsley—that's one awkward night waiting to happen. And I really want to get back home. My head hurts and I've got to figure out a way to get the barn cleaned up. I don't know what we'll do if we have to repaint. It's not cheap."

I bit my lip and thought for a second. "Tell you what, you don't worry about that paint. I'll take care of it for you."

"Ains."

I held up a hand. "It's the least I can do. You don't worry about it. But I do need to buy three or four bottles of wine."

She smiled. It didn't quite reach her eyes, but she guided me to the front of the barn where they sold wine and did the tastings.

Danny watched us as we made our way around. He was good-looking with his blond curls and dark brown eyes and he had a nice smile.

"Hey, Shannon, I'll catch up with you in just a bit. I need some Chardonnay and the Cabernet. I just wanted to ask Danny something real quick."

Either he'd help me determine if the murder weapon came from the winery or I'd get to use my creep radar up close and personal to ferret out his motives for coming to Sweet River at just the right time to see Rick murdered.

He glanced up and smiled. I returned it. He really was a handsome man.

"Hi, I won't keep you," I said as I made my way through the vines. "I just had a quick favor to ask."

"Whatever you need." His voice was light and friendly. He did seem to be a nice guy. Whew. The last thing Shannon and Michael needed was someone taking advantage.

"Great. Would it be possible for you to take a look and see if any of the bottles of wine are missing? Like maybe there is an inventory list or something?"

His eyebrows drew together. "The police asked for the same thing. I made copies of everything and we did a count. Nothing was missing—at least as far as we can tell."

"Okay great. I just didn't know if we needed to count the crates we have in the back or something. Thanks."

"No problem."

I started to walk away and then stopped. I turned around to find him still watching me.

"One more thing: Shannon says you guys have been friends for a long time."

He pulled the shears out from his belt. "We have been, probably six years. I'm really proud of all that Michael has accomplished."

"Me, too. Do you know anyone who might want to frame him like this?"

Danny shook his head. "No. You know him—he's the nicest guy I ever met. When we used to work together, he gave me one of his best accounts. And then when he left, to start his business, he made sure all of his clients asked for me. I owe him everything."

"That sounds like him." This guy didn't sound like a killer any more than Michael. Time to move on. "Thanks for helping them. I don't know what Shannon would do right now otherwise."

He shrugged. "No place I'd rather be."

I waved goodbye and went to find Shannon.

Now, all I had to do was convince my brother to tell me everything he knew about the case without him realizing that was what he was doing. And it had to be in front of his friends.

Sigh.

Shannon handed me the bag of wine, each bottle carefully wrapped. She was wearier than I'd ever seen her.

I was going into the lion's den, but I'd do anything for my best friend.

Anything.

Chapter Seven

BY THE TIME my brother and his friends showed up, the lasagna was almost done. I had a bottle of wine uncorked. I might have had a sip or two for liquid courage. My brother's favorite beer was in the fridge and a cherry pie was ready to go in the oven when the lasagna came out.

The guys walked in without knocking. They'd only been out to my house a few times. We had a Friendsgiving Thanksgiving night a year ago for people who might not have family in town, and for a few who did. We, my brother and I, made enough to take to the officers working the holiday shift at the station.

But most of the time, my brother is the entertainer. He likes to barbeque all summer and our friends tend to congregate around his fire pit in his backyard. We only use my place if we need a bigger space.

"George Clooney, give me five," Jake said. It was one of the few tricks George deemed worthy of learning. He stuck out a paw and then rumbled something.

"Is that so? I'll see what I can do."

My brother laughed. "What did he ask?"

"What? You didn't understand him? It was perfectly clear. He said Ainsley's lasagna smells delicious and he wants a piece."

I laughed. I couldn't help it.

"Hey, guys, there's wine on the counter and beer in the fridge."

"What do you guys want?" Kane asked as he walked in behind my brother. "And, Ainsley, I brought some of my mom's homemade garlic bread. She sent some home to put in the freezer last time I was there."

"Beer," my brother said. No surprise there.

"If the wine is from Michael's place, I'll try whatever you have opened," Jake said.

Kane handed me the foil-wrapped package.

"Thanks, I hadn't put mine in yet. I can't wait to taste this. Homemade is always so much better than store bought."

He nodded. After grabbing the drinks, he headed toward his friends.

I put the bread in and was chopping a salad when Jake came into the kitchen.

"Is there anything I can do to help?"

The oven dinged. "There are some pot holders over there if you want to get the lasagna out for me—and the bread. You can just set them on the stove for right now to cool."

"Got it. Everything really does smell amazing. Thanks for making us a meal tonight."

"You're welcome."

"So is this some kind of plot to get information from your brother?"

I stopped chopping the tomato. "Uh. I don't know what you mean."

He chuckled. "Dave works with me at the fire station.

His aunt is Ms. Helen who is a member of the book club."

"Oh." Darn that woman and her mouth.

"She mentioned to him that you and your friends were putting together a suspect board."

I kind of wanted to slam my head against the cabinet at that point. It was dumb that I ever thought we could keep things quiet.

I sighed, and he chuckled again. "You should tell your brother what you guys have heard. Michael doesn't deserve what's happening to him. I've been friends for years with Greg and Michael. It's ripping Greg up, but he's doing what he must."

"I know but I don't feel like the police, in general, are really trying that hard."

"What?" Greg asked.

Crud. He and Kane were standing in front of the breakfast bar. I thought they'd been a bit further away by George. The whole downstairs was an open concept, but it was a big space.

Once again, I had a serious case of foot-in-mouth disease.

"I only mean, that you have your suspect and evidence, and there seems to be a reluctance to look at anyone else, even though you know he didn't do it."

My brother's eyebrow went up, which was never a good sign. "Ainsley, he's my friend. I'm doing everything I can to get him out of there."

"So, you don't believe he did it." He had no idea how important the answer to that question was to me.

"Of course, I don't. But the evidence is there, and all of

the other suspects have alibis. He had a bail hearing. I don't understand why he's deciding to stay in lockup."

It was such a relief to hear him say those words about Michael's innocence. "Wait, there are other suspects?"

Greg frowned and then glanced up at the ceiling like he was asking heaven for patience. "Yes, Ainsley. We are looking into all the leads."

There was an uncomfortable silence. I finished chopping the last bit of tomato. I like my salads in bite-sized pieces.

"And he's staying in lockup because he doesn't want anyone to be financially responsible for him. Not that he'd go on the run. But he doesn't want anyone's money. That's the kind of guy you have in jail."

Another uncomfortable silence. It might be a while before my brother accepted another invitation from me to hang out again.

"Greg, can you take this salad to the table?" I asked more to change the subject than anything.

"I've got the lasagna," Jake said.

"If you've got something to put the bread in, I can take care of that," Kane added.

Nothing like an argument with siblings to throw a damper on the night. I handed Kane a basket for the bread. I'd already set the table, so we put all the food in the middle and passed it around family style, except for the lasagna, which I served.

The guys chatted about football and basketball. The police and fire stations were sponsoring a charity event for the basketball program for kids in need.

I jumped up when I realized I'd forgotten to put the

cherry pie in the oven.

"Do you need help with anything?" Jake asked again as he followed me into the kitchen. He was so polite.

"Just putting the pie in the oven."

"You need to tell him what you guys found out, Ainsley."

Those gorgeous eyes of his, well, it felt like they could see right through me.

"I don't want to ruin the dinner. I feel like I've put you guys through enough and I really am sorry about that."

"Nothing to be sorry about. Your brother is one of my best friends and will be for life, but you might find Kane and I are pretty good allies for you. We're worried about the same thing. Kane's been working double shifts trying to find some other evidence to prove Michael's innocence. So don't worry about us. We're just as interested in what you have to say, as you are in finding out what Greg knows."

For the first time in days, I smiled. A genuine one. "Thanks. But get ready because he is most likely going to rip my head off. It's like poking a bear lately with him."

"We can take it. And he's under a lot of stress. Like I said earlier, Michael's his friend, too."

I knew that. But it didn't make it any easier to start that line of questioning with my brother.

I cleared my throat as I sat back down. "I meant to tell you earlier, there was some vandalism out at Michael's place." I explained about the lettering.

"Why didn't Shannon call me?"

I didn't want to hurt his feelings, so I just stared at my lasagna.

"Oh," he said softly. "Well, it's a crime and even if she is angry with me, she should report it. I'll go take a look as soon as we're done with dinner."

"Thanks," I said.

"Greg, let me know when you're done looking into it," Jake said. "Then I'll take some of the guys over tomorrow morning and see if we can power wash the paint off," Jake said.

"And there's something else I need to tell you." *But I really don't want to.*

He put his fork down and took a sip of his beer. "If it's about your murder board, I already know. Erma's nephew works at the station."

Well, that was sort of a relief. "Did they tell you what we'd discovered?"

"No," he said flatly.

I told him everything from the wife's vacation to the girlfriend being very rude. All of it.

"I think, what we're doing—sometimes people may not want to talk to the police like they would a friend or neighbor. I'm quite certain you aren't happy with my snooping, but I made a promise to Shannon to help any way I can."

"Ainsley, you think a group of amateur detectives are better at solving a case than the police?"

I sighed for the fourth time that night. "No. Please don't get defensive. I need you to hear what I'm saying. I'm just asking folks questions and that's what the book club gang is doing. We all love Michael, and none of us likes the idea that there's still a killer running around. And you're really busy with the fall festival, and the college homecoming. I'm just asking that you let us be the ears for you. Like a community patrol or something."

He rubbed his forehead and then pinched the bridge of his nose. "You're going to do this whether I approve or not, aren't you?"

I bit my lip and then nodded.

"Fine. I'm going on record as saying I do not like this at all. I'm worried you might get hurt. As you said, there could still be a killer on the loose. But don't do anything stupid or dangerous. You're all I have left."

I reached over and patted his hand. "Any chance I could see your police files?" I grinned.

"Ains, it's an active police investigation. That would be a no."

"Okay. Okay. I had to ask."

The guys chuckled.

The oven dinged again. I started gathering plates, but the guys picked up their own and followed me into the kitchen. "I'm guessing you all want pie?"

"Yes," they said in unison.

"Coffee and cups are over there if you want some. And, Greg, can you get the ice cream out of the fridge?"

We took everything back to the table and I served them on my fiesta ware I'd picked up at the Round Top Antiques Fair earlier in the fall. I'd bought all different colors and liked to mismatch them with my place settings. It's the little things like that, that keep me happy.

An hour later, they were all set to go.

Kane was the last to leave.

"Hey, can I ask you a few things?"

He glanced outside and then back at me. Then he shut the door.

"Sure. But if it's about the case, I'm not sure I can share. My work falls under the same guidelines as your brother's."

"Right. I get that. I'm just curious why all the evidence points to Michael when there are so many other suspects. You heard what I said. They all had motive, something Michael didn't have." Unless he'd found out about the victim hitting on Shannon. But I wouldn't even let my mind go there. Even if he had known, it wouldn't have been a reason to murder the guy. I did leave that part of my explanation out when I told Greg "everything."

"I can't tell you much, but the force it took to kill someone with a wine bottle like that, well, it had to be someone tall and strong. Michael is both. From what I understand, it just wouldn't be possible for most of the other suspects to do that. It's actually very hard to kill someone like that. The bottle broke in such a way that one of the shards cut the stem of the brain. It's odd because the skull is a great protector and hard to break through."

Well crud. That was exactly what I didn't want to hear.

If we were going to help Michael, we had to find someone with motive and the strength to have killed the victim.

His wife and girlfriend had alibis. And Danny Avery hadn't been in town and would do anything for Shannon and Michael.

I sat down next to George Clooney on the couch.

Then it hit me. Instead of thinking about who tried to the kill the victim, maybe I should focus on a different tack. That wine bottle had been very specific.

Who would want to frame Michael for murder?

Chapter Eight

O N THE WAY to work the next morning, I drove past Jake and his firemen friends washing the letters off of Michael's barn. The kindness I witnessed had me blinking away tears. Knowing that Jake and Kane, and even my brother, believed in Michael's innocence, made me feel better about life.

But we had to prove it.

I was all the way to the store before I realized it was Sunday. I laughed as George stared at me in the rearview mirror. I was so set in my routine and so caught up in who might want to frame Michael, I forgot what day it was.

"Well, we're here. Let's run some reports to see how we did last week, and make sure everything is ready to reopen on Tuesday." We'd collectively decided to only be open five days a week. Since it was a small town in Texas and a lot of folks did the church thing, Sunday was an easy decision. And to give our vendors a good break we all decided on Monday, as well.

"Maybe, I'll set a reminder to sleep in tomorrow."

George grunted as he followed me to the front counter. I booted up the computer and ran some sales reports. I'm a bit OCD about numbers and it's important for me to make this business thrive, not just for me, but for everyone involved.

These people went along with my dream and they deserved to achieve theirs, as well.

A half hour later, I printed everything and shoved the papers into my messenger bag. "Let's go get some coffee and then we'll head home."

I clipped George's leash to one of the patio tables outside, and went in to order. I was surprised to see Shannon at the register. The cozy shop buzzed with the church crowd either going to or coming from their place of worship. Dressed in an old T-shirt, sweater and jeans, I was a bit out of place amid all the Sunday best.

"I thought you took Sundays off? Is someone sick?"

She made my coffee and then brought it to me. "No. But I can only clean my house so many times. I needed something to get me out of my head."

"Sorry."

She shrugged. "I'm trying to stay positive and keep moving. By the way, I talked to your brother this morning."

"Oh?"

"Thanks for sending him my way." I hadn't done that exactly, and I honestly couldn't tell if she was being sarcastic.

"Well, a crime was committed." I parroted what Greg had said the day before.

"Funny. That's what he said. We actually had a good chat and I feel bad about being so angry toward him. He is caught in the middle. And he promised to try and talk some sense into my fiancé. There's absolutely no reason for him to stay behind bars. I mean money is tight, but it's only ten percent. I'm one hundred percent willing to put the coffee shop up as collateral. I believe in him that much."

I've never experienced the kind of bond she had with Michael. Sure, I've dated, but the guys always end up being jerks. I've sort of given up on that part of my life. I'm focused on my new career as an entrepreneur, and it's a lot more rewarding.

"Well, if you want, I'm always happy to stop by and visit him. I don't know that he'll listen to me any more than he would you or Greg, but I'm happy to try. I asked my brother if I could bring cookies or something and visit and he said it would be all right."

"If Greg can't get through to him, I might take you up on that."

I paid for my coffee. "Don't work too hard, and if you want to come over later, we could do a girls' spa day. Goodness knows I need a manicure and I haven't had time to get to Nellie's Nails in more than month. And I bought some of those moisturizing face masks that are supposed to take ten years off immediately."

Shannon smiled and this time it reached her eyes. "Yes. That sounds wonderful. I'll bring wine and food. And I have some wild new polishes I picked out a few weeks ago that I've been dying to try."

I'm more of a nude or light pink person, but if it made her smile, I'd do anything.

"Sounds like a plan."

LATER THAT NIGHT, I waited for Shannon. George Clooney was in his favorite sleeping position on the couch. He'd spent the last twenty minutes doing his wild dog thing out in the backyard and was exhausted.

I was in the kitchen making some strawberry shortcake. It's a summer dish for most people, but in South Texas strawberries are in season most of the year. But the main reason I was neck deep in mixing the whip cream? It was Shannon's favorite. And she could absolutely use a bit of a break and a bit of looking after.

When she pulled up in her car into the drive, George Clooney raised his head and woofed.

"Thanks, awesome guard dog."

I swear he grumbled under his breath as he went back to sleep. I was kind of amazed at his ability to know friend from foe, especially from the sound of their car or truck.

One of his many talents.

I brushed the crumbs from my hands into the sink and met her at the door.

We hugged and then she followed me to the breakfast bar. "I know it's sacrilege to say, since I'm a winemaker's fiancée, but I wasn't in the mood to drink. I brought some stuff to make my Harry Potter Butterbeer, the non-alcoholic kind."

"You had me at butter," I said. "I made you some strawberry shortcake."

Shannon loved strawberry shortcake. She had mentioned her mom used to make it nearly every Sunday night and Shannon went nuts for the homemade whipped cream.

She laughed. "You really are the best friend. It's kind of an odd combo, maybe I should have brought something a little bit lighter."

"Nah. If you don't care, I don't care. It's all sweet and that's what I'm in the mood for tonight. Do you want to eat or do nails first?"

She grinned, and it was good to see. I had missed that smile while away in Chicago, but now it was like we'd never been apart. "What do you think?"

After we ate and chatted about her new fall menu for the coffee shop, we pulled out our nail stuff. Well, I should say, she pulled out a kit with just about every color I could imagine.

Shannon was always prepared. That was the reason she'd earned so many badges in Girl Scouts and the main reason she ran such a successful business today.

She was there for me when my parents died, quietly supporting me in a million ways I didn't fully comprehend until much later. Our friendship was cemented then and has withstood moves, exes, long-distance calls, and more.

"Wow. That's quite the collection."

"Well, some people collect shoes and purses, I'm a nail polish kind of girl. I change them at least once a week. Sometimes more because my hands are in water so much. When I glance down at my fingernails, it can brighten my mood to see the color."

"I know that this is going to come as a huge shock to you, but I usually wear clear or a very light pink."

She squinted at me and pursed her lips. "Ainsley McGregor, you're trying to say you're boring or not so brave, but you are. Look what you've done with the artisanal market? It took courage for you to take a chance on something you'd never done before, and it's paying off, right?"

"Well, it's only the first week but so far so good." I didn't mention the murder, one she knew much too well. "I'm hoping, since we're at the beginning of Christmas season, it will continue."

"Oh, that reminds me," she said as she picked up one bottle and then put it down. "I'm on the street-decorating committee. I'm supposed to ask if you want wreaths with the traditional red and gold balls, or all white."

I loved this woman. "You told them they needed to do white, didn't you, to match my building?"

She shrugged. "I think it's good to shake things up. You have the biggest building, so it's up to you. I just thought white ribbon and gold balls, or even white and red balls would be so pretty. We'll do the traditional greenery and garland across the streets and on the gas lampposts."

Those lamps were one of my favorite things about Main Street.

"Actually, the white might look kind of dirty after a few days with all the dust around here," I said practically.

Her eyes opened wide. "Oh, I didn't even think about that. That's a great point."

"But thank you for thinking of me. If they haven't done the ordering yet, maybe think about doing the dark green with the red balls. That traditional look is great on just about everything. I'll make sure we do some fun window displays to liven things up."

I'd found an animatronic Santa that was a good foot taller than me. I just needed to find someone to rewire him. We could hang garland around the big rafters and each booth could have its own—

Fingers snapped in front of my face.

"Hello?" Shannon laughed. It was a lovely sound. "Your head is turning with decorating ideas, isn't it?"

I grinned right back. "It's like you know me or something."

She waved a bottle in front of my eyes. "This is the perfect color for fall. It's called oxblood and it's gorgeous on."

"It's very red."

"Yes, almost black. I promise you'll love it. Let me put it on." She removed my old polish, filed my short nails to smooth out the rough spots, and then rubbed some delicious-smelling oil on my hands.

"Marry me," I said as I closed my eyes. That hand massage was the most relaxing thing I'd done in weeks.

"I'm spoken for," she said and then sighed.

My eyes popped open. *Way to go. Remind her of the sad stuff why don't you.*

"I'm so sorry."

She shook her head. "Stop. We're having fun. And if ever I want a platonic marriage, I promise you'll be the first person I call."

"Same," I said.

"Now go wash off all the goo and I'll paint them."

An hour later we both had new nails. She'd chosen a burnt orange for her. I had to admit, I did like the oxblood.

We were about to pop in a movie and do face masks when George Clooney jumped off the couch and ran to the back door. It was the same menacing growl I'd heard a few nights ago.

"George. Shhh."

"What's all that about?" Shannon asked.

"I think there's an animal out in the woods. This happened the other night."

George pawed at the door.

"Shhhhh." I rubbed his head and tried to calm him down. "Probably a raccoon or maybe a coyote but you are not going outside." No way I'd risk him getting hurt.

"Do you think someone might be back there?"

That was the big question and it was one I'd been considering.

I hoped not. But I did feel like someone was watching me the other night.

I flipped on the back porch light. I couldn't see anything. Shannon joined me and peered out the French doors leading off the kitchen.

George calmed down. I gave him one of his bones to chew on. Normally, he'd head back to the couch and his blanket. But he settled on the rug by the French doors as if he were on lookout or something.

Nerves coursed through me like a raging river.

Could someone be out there?

Shannon put a hand on my shoulder. "I'm sure everything is fine. He's settled down. Let's go watch a movie. Besides, you promised these face masks would make me look ten years younger."

I glanced away from the door. This night was about her. "That's what the box says."

"Do you ever get scared out here by yourself? I mean, the nearest house is probably Jake's and he's at least a mile away."

I hadn't ever been scared, well, until the last few nights. George and I had lived here a year, and he'd never been on edge like that. "No. I like the quiet. Besides, I don't think there'd be a yard big enough for George in town."

She bent down and petted his head. "You are one amazing dog, George, but you're huge. I still can't believe she brought you home from the shelter."

A few minutes after we finished with the face masks, which were way more goopy than expected, we were snuggled in blankets on the couch and watching a movie. George sauntered in, did his three-circle thing on the end of the sofa and then lay down.

I guess the threat is gone. Had to have been some kind of animal.

"This movie is way more fun than I expected," she said.

I'd found the latest romantic comedy on the streaming service. It was light and fun—exactly what we both needed.

When it was over, she yawned. "Do you mind if I sleep on your couch? I'm so sleepy all of a sudden."

"I finally got the guest room fixed up last month. You can sleep there. You even have your own bathroom."

That had been the last of the home renovations, which was good. I was almost out of money. The only thing I had left to do was to get the air-conditioning and heat out into the sunroom on the side of the house. George loved hanging out in there, probably because it was all windows and he could run from the back of the house to the front, surveying the land.

I made sure Shannon had towels and gave her one of my ginormous T-shirts I liked to sleep in. It said, "Girl, please. I ride a unicorn." It was one of my gifts from a professor friend when I left the University of Chicago.

Sometimes that life seemed a hundred years away. This time of year, it would already be so chilly. I much preferred the Texas warmth.

"We need to get some more of these T-shirts. We could wear them to the fall festival in a couple of weeks. Michael and I—" She bit her lip. "I almost forgot he probably won't be going to the festival. Ainsley, this is all so unfair." She sat down on the edge of the bed, holding the shirt to her chest.

My heart tugged and I hurt for her.

"Look. He's innocent. And no matter what, his dad's fancy lawyer is going to get him off the hook. I don't like any of this or how it's going down. But we will figure it out. I'm here for you and Michael. He's staying in because he believes in the system. I do too. I just think the system could use an extra set of eyes and ears."

She took a deep breath. "I think your murder board could help."

I shook my head. "For something that was supposed to be secret, it seems the whole world knows at this point. And we just started it Friday night. Even my brother found out."

"I bet he was happy about that."

"He thinks I'm nuts and that it's dumb for amateurs to even try. But then I told him some of the other things we'd heard around town. Like other people whose stories seemed suspicious. He's promised to look into everything."

She nodded. "He told me when he stopped by that he was doing everything he could. Like I said before, I believe him. I would like to be in on the meetings. I mean, I was going to come for book club the other night, but I was worried what people might think. You know, if I was out painting the town while my poor fiancé is in jail."

I rolled my eyes. "Book club is hardly painting the town. We've decided to meet weekly for a bit, so there is one next Friday. But please beware, we spend about a half hour talking about books and then the other hour and a half discussing who should go on the board."

"I'm up for anything that isn't work or sitting in my house waiting for answers."

"Great. I'll text it to you later. Get some sleep. You've got a long day tomorrow."

"Are you teaching at the university in the morning?"

Since the shop was closed on Mondays, that's when I taught my grad school class on popular literature. Thankfully, tomorrow they were pretty much turning in papers and we had a short lecture about the Dan Brown and James Patterson effect. Writing short chapters to move the story forward and keeping the attention of readers. It was more difficult to write that way because every chapter needed a strong prompt at the beginning and a hook at the end. I'd tried writing a novel a couple of times, but I was much better off dissecting what made them work.

"Yes. But I promise to stop by the station early tomorrow to see what I can find out. Now you get some rest. Those masks won't do us any good if we don't sleep."

She giggled a little. "I do feel like they helped a lot."

"Me too. Night."

"Night."

"Ainsley?"

I turned around to face her. "Yes?"

"Thank you for everything. I don't have any other friends like you. One, who—'There aren't many people who would go around questioning strangers and trying to figure out who the killer is."

"I don't know if that makes me a good friend or just nuts. Also, I have done mostly gathering of info and putting it all in one place. You can thank Ms. Helen and Ms. Erma. Those two women—they are a force for sure."

"True. Thanks again for everything."

"I'm doing exactly what you would do for me."

George rustled around downstairs. "I'm going to check on George. Let me know if you need anything else."

He was restless, pacing by the back door. He wasn't growling so I let him out. Maybe he hadn't finished his business earlier. But then he went for the fence line acting like a crazy mutt.

"Hey, stop that."

As much as I didn't want to go outside, I stepped out onto the back porch.

"If someone is out there, please go away. I can't promise he won't try to jump the fence and bite." I have no idea why I said that. Whatever was out there upset George.

Okay, and freaked me out in a major way.

I don't like guns but right then, I sort of wish I had one for show. My Spidey sense—I'd had no idea I had it—was off the charts. Someone was out there. I was about to grab my phone and call Greg, when George Clooney stopped and trotted back to me like nothing had happened.

Ugh. "I'm glad you're all nice and calm, I want to throw

up I'm so nervous."

Maybe it was just an animal.

I closed all the blinds in the house and then turned on the lights downstairs. I wanted to haul George upstairs with me, but after grabbing a drink out of his bowl, he did his three turns and settled down on the sofa.

There was no way I could go to sleep. I ran upstairs and changed into my PJs, and then settled on the couch next to George.

I was mad more than anything else. For the first time since moving to Texas, someone had made me afraid in my own house.

That would not do.

"You'll protect, me, won't you, boy? And I'll do the same for you."

He grunted and then put his head in my lap.

In the light of day, I'd do some investigating out by the woods. Maybe it was just some kids messing around. Or it might be an animal like I'd thought earlier.

But my senses told me otherwise.

When I stopped by to see my brother the next day, I'd mention it to him. Maybe he'd know if there was some kind of hangout or something in the woods behind my house.

What if it's the killer and he isn't happy that you're messing around with the case?

Yep. Sleep most definitely would not be my friend.

Chapter Nine

B LEARY-EYED THE NEXT morning, I threw my rain boots over my pajamas and went to investigate the acreage that butts up against the woods. Shannon had left hours before, and bless her, had put the coffee on.

Around three, I'd fallen asleep next to George Clooney. That dog snores so loud, but it was comforting in a way. We were up by seven and since he needed out anyway, I let him into the fenced backyard, while I checked the property line.

If there were animals, I didn't want him chasing after them. I've never hoped so hard that it was some sort of creature making him nuts. It was quiet and chilly. I put the baseball bat I was carrying—it was the only thing close to a weapon I had—in the crook of my arm and zipped up my hoodie. Pulled the hood up over my ears.

I'd just reached the tree line when George barked. Maybe I screamed a little. Oh, and the best part? I dropped the bat on my toe. Yep, it was a very good thing I didn't have a gun.

"Ouch." I turned to tell George to hush when I saw him.

Jake, more handsome than any man had a right to be, was headed around the fenced area calling out a greeting to George who dutifully ran up to get a pat on the head. It was a chain-link fence and both George and Jake were very tall, so they had no problem with that.

"Hey," I said. "What's up?"

I was dressed in my favorite unicorn pajama bottoms, bright pink rain boots and aforementioned hoodie. No makeup. Thank goodness my hair was covered. I hadn't bothered to look in a mirror, but rats' nest, I'm fairly certain, was not the latest hairstyle in *Vogue*.

It didn't matter. This guy was so out of my league.

"Your brother stopped at the coffee shop and said you guys had a problem last night. That you were worried someone was in the woods. He's busy this morning with another case and asked if I could come check it out."

I hadn't texted my brother, so how did he know? *Maybe Shannon told him?* I'm sure she woke up with all the racket.

"Um. Well, George did go a little nuts. And a few days ago, same thing. He's never done anything like that. Ever. But I'm sure it's just an animal or something."

He shrugged. "Well, I'm here. Let's have a look."

I followed him to the tree line.

"Did you see anything?"

"No. I mean, maybe it was my imagination, but it felt like something or someone was watching the house. But who would be out in these woods?"

"Well, they're not supposed to be this close to rural areas with homes, but it could be hunters," Jake said as he stooped down to look at something in the grass. "It's deer season and we've had an overpopulation. Not my thing but we have a lot of hunters in the area. Still, they wouldn't be out that late at night."

Oh. No. *Bambi* scarred me for life. I couldn't imagine anyone killing one of those sweet, docile animals. I squeezed my arms around my waist.

"I don't like guns," I said as if that resolved all the world's problems.

"They have their place, but they aren't for everyone. Your brother needs his for his job. Couldn't pay me to be a cop these days."

"Jake?"

He turned away from the trees to glance at me. "Yeah?"

"You run into burning buildings. That seems a whole lot scarier."

He chuckled. "Point well made. But with fires, you have a general idea of what you're running into. Being a cop, you never know when someone is going to come at you. And right now, your poor brother is understaffed. He's been pulling double shifts for weeks."

I had no idea. Maybe that's why he'd been so cranky lately.

"I know you're really busy, too, so thanks for coming out here at the crack of dawn."

"Ainsley, you know I'd do anything for you and your brother." He turned back to the woods.

My hand flew to my chest. And my brain went straight to *anything*?

Ainsley McGregor, stop that. First, he's your brother's best friend. Goes against the code.

Greg couldn't date my friends and I couldn't date his. We'd made that pact in puberty when I'd caught him giving Darla, my BFF at the time, the eyebrow. But that went both ways.

And Jake was so out of my league. Like I'm Little

League, maybe a T-ball player, and he's a pitcher in the majors.

That is the extent of my knowledge of sports.

I'm not a troll but his type was more homecoming queen and I fall along the lines of art nerd.

I absolutely, one hundred percent, could never think of Jake as anything more than a friend.

Right. Keeping telling yourself that. Sometimes my conscience was a pain.

"Huh," he said.

"Is that a good huh or a bad one?"

He knelt down and took a picture of something on the ground. "There are definitely some footprints back here. But I have no idea when they were made."

A chill skidded down my spine, straight to my hands, which I balled into fists to stop them from shaking.

"Oh?" I didn't know what to say. Some stranger had been back here watching my house.

"It's not a boot print. It's sneakers, I can tell from the imprint of the sole. I'll text it to your brother."

"Why would they be out here?" It didn't make sense. "I mean, I could see if it was hunters, maybe, but they don't wear sneakers."

"Probably just some kids running around. But it's best to be sure. Do you have security in the house?" He was still on the ground and shadowed his face with his hand as he glanced up at me.

"No. I mean, we live in such a small town and everyone leaves their doors unlocked. I—" It's dumb because I'd been living in Chicago for years before moving to Sweet River.

And while Chi town is a wonderful place, it can be a dangerous one as well. No one knew that better than me. I'd been mugged twice. After the second time, my brother convinced me to move here the day after he checked me out of the hospital. I'd finished out the term. Given up my tenure, the youngest professor ever to have it in that department and moved back to Texas.

And I hadn't regretted it until just now.

"Jake, you're scaring me."

He stood then and put a hand on my shoulder, the warmth of him seeping through the hoodie. "I don't mean to. For the most part, Sweet River is one of the safest towns you'll ever find. You heard what people said, it's been years since we've had a murder. But it isn't Mayfield. But we have a lot of tourists, and that's an unknown element. You have to be careful. You're a woman out here alone in the middle of the country. At the very least, you need a security system."

I rubbed the bridge of my nose with my fingers. All of this was just too much. Murder and people watching my place. If that was what was happening. He'd said those prints could have been made any time.

No way I'd let my imagination run away and think the worst.

"You don't like guns, but you might want to look into a stun gun. They have some very safe ones that are simple to use. And out here in the country, you might have to run off a coyote or two, so a BB gun might also be something to look in to. Usually the sound is enough to scare them. You don't want George getting into a fight with one of those guys."

I sighed. "I'll talk to Greg and see what he thinks. Did you already send him the picture?"

He nodded.

"Great. I'll be in for the 'you'd be much better off in town' speech. But I won't do that to George."

"I don't blame you," he said as he let go of my shoulder. "I've lived out here for more than ten years and never had any trouble. All of this is probably nothing. Don't be scared. But maybe let's look into getting you set up with some security and a way to protect yourself for the just in cases. At least some lights for out here, and a system for the house."

I nodded.

George barked. "I better go feed him. That dog loves his routine. Breakfast at eight thirty every morning on the dot or there is hell to pay."

Jake's laugh sent a different kind of chill down my spine. *No, Ainsley. Bad girl. No.*

"Okay. We'll, I'm going to look around here a bit more. See you later."

"Thanks," I said as I waved goodbye.

FORTY-FIVE MINUTES LATER, I was at the station. Kevin was working the front desk again.

"Is my brother in?"

"He said for you and George to wait in his office. He's out on a domestic dispute but says he'll be back soon."

George and I went into the office. As usual, the desk was piled high with file folders. The one with the murder case just happened to be open on his desk. The pictures on top were so gruesome but I couldn't look away. It was weird. Part of me kept forgetting this was a real guy. This wasn't a game or a murder in a book. He was a person with a wife and a mistress. Maybe he wasn't the nicest dude in the world, but no one deserved to be murdered.

You shouldn't look at the files.

But I really wanted to. In the worst sort of way.

I sat down across from his desk in one of the black chairs. After about two minutes, I couldn't stand it. I mean, he knew I was coming by. Maybe he wanted me to see what was going on without witnessing it. Why else would he leave them out on the desk like that?

I started thumbing through them. I wished I hadn't. The work the police had put into this made my little murder board seem useless.

I discovered the wine bottle used as the murder weapon was a Chardonnay. From the scene photo, I could tell that it didn't have the price tag from Bless Your Art, so it was more likely to have come directly from the winery. And who had direct access to the winery's inventory? Danny? Michael? Several workers, and possibly Shannon.

That said, there were notations in the file of the things I had told my brother. In fact, he'd already had someone checking into when the wife's Maldives tickets were bought.

The mistress was another story. Evidently, he'd promised to take her back to Brazil where her family lived. She swore she had no idea that the victim had been married. That she believed they had a common law marriage. But there was a note in my brother's handwriting that he didn't believe her.

There was no way the mistress could live in the town and have no idea he was married. And there was something fishy, as in she had very few details about the victim. She kept stating she was too distraught to think, but my brother had written in all caps: LYING.

Interesting.

She'd said he traveled a lot for business. There was a note that her alibi was exactly the same as the wife's. Something felt off about that. Both women in crowded restaurants with lots of witnesses. One in Fredericksburg, which was a town just a bit west of Sweet River, and one in Round Top, which was a bit east.

My brother was right. That did feel off.

I was just about to peek at the autopsy report when I heard my brother's voice. I took a quick picture with my phone of that and some of the other files and then sat down quickly.

"Hey," he says.

"Hey."

"You know what I'm going to say, don't you?" He sat down behind his desk.

"Yes. So, skip the lecture."

The wrinkles around his eyes were a little deeper than when I'd seen him on Saturday.

"Is everything all right?"

He shrugged. "Just a lot going on with the festival and people seem to be a bit jumpy these days."

"Kevin said you had a domestic dispute. What was that about?"

He glanced up at the ceiling and then down at his desk.

"It's police business. You know I can't discuss things like that with you."

"Does it have anything to do with the case against Michael? If it does, I'd appreciate it if you told me. I mean, did what I told you the other night help?"

He frowned as if he knew I'd been snooping, but then he shrugged.

He sighed. "Fine. But we're not going to make a habit of sharing details about a case, okay?"

"Since this is the only case I'm ever going to care about, deal."

"And you'll promise to tell me if you hear anything through the Ainsley McGregor network? I've been investigating some of those leads you gave me."

I started to say, I know, but I checked myself. "Oh? Well good. Maybe something will help. I made a promise to Shannon to assist whatever way I could. And you know this town better than I do. People like to gossip, but there may be some truths in there."

"Agreed."

"So, what was the domestic dispute?"

"The mistress says she is pregnant. She showed up at the lawyer's office when the wife was there, demanding half of the estate for her child. There was a bit of hair pulling and a lot of screaming. I threatened to bring them both in, and that seemed to cool them down."

I leaned back in my chair. "Wow. If that's not motive to kill someone, I don't know what is."

"Well, maybe if she'd killed the wife. But why kill him? The provider?"

I remembered his notes. "What if the wife or the mistress found out about the other?"

He frowned. "First thing we looked into. They both have airtight alibis with witnesses. And when Lucy told the wife about the mistress, I was watching. Her jaw dropped and there was so much anger."

"Hmmm. I'd like to see Michael. I brought him some cinnamon rolls and coffee. I brought some for you, too." I pointed to the cup and the small white bag on his desk.

"I can ask him, but it will have to be later. His fancy lawyer is with him right now."

I scrunched up my face. "I promised Shannon I'd talk some sense into him today."

"Pretty sure that's what his lawyer is trying to do. I hope it works. The district attorney is pushing for me to send him to the larger county lockup, and I don't want to do that. It's not as bad as some prisons but it's no place for a good guy like Michael. This is a five-star hotel compared to that place."

I leaned back in the uncomfortable metal chair with the worn cushion. "I'd wondered how he was able to stay in here for so long. I mean, not that I have that much experience with this sort of stuff. But usually you guys process them right out."

He nodded. "But when we know someone is innocent, it makes it a little harder."

"See that's what I don't get. I thought he was innocent until proven guilty."

"In theory that's always true. But the case against him is solid. I told you before, I don't like it any more than you do."

"I know. I know. Well, I guess I can stop by again later. If the lawyer doesn't work. Is it okay if I text you on my way back from the college?"

"Sure. And about that security issue at your place."

I'd hoped he'd forgotten about that.

"I've sent the team out to take some casts of the footprints. I've called Dave, who set up your security for the store. He's going to put in motion sensor lights, cameras, the whole shebang." He held up a hand when I tried to speak. "It's my treat. And the alarm will be loud enough we can hear it all the way into town. Until then, you can stay at my place."

"Nope. That's not going to happen. You know I won't do that to George."

At the sound of his name, he'd raised his head as if to nod.

My brother chuckled. "Fine. But you're going to keep all the doors and windows locked. You will call me if you suspect anything. And I mean, right away. Don't blow it off. I'll also be sending a patrol by several times a night. We've been needing to keep a better eye on the rural areas anyway. It's a good start. I'm also picking you up a stun gun. No arguments."

I held up my hands like I was giving up. "Fine." I'd probably end up hurting myself with it, but if it made him feel better, I'd take it.

But I wasn't scared anymore. Anger scorched through my blood. I would not be frightened out of my home.

By the time I'd reached the university, it was nearly time for my class. I took George on a quick walk and gave him some food and water in the small office I kept there.

Sweet River College of Fine Arts was a private school, which was well funded thanks to some Texas oil barons. But the kids who went there, at least the ones in the grad school where I taught, were far from entitled. They were rich kids, but ones interested in creating a better future. They were more politically and saving-the-world driven than any class I'd ever had before. But even more exciting—they were always eager to explore new ideas.

It's the only reason I kept this one day of teaching. That and they offered health insurance for part-timers. Dean Slay, who was the head of the English department, was one of my favorite humans on the planet. She was the first one to push me toward opening the shop and insisted that I stay on. "You're too talented and too good of a professor. These kids need you. You know you'll miss it if you give it up entirely."

The *kids* were mostly adults in their early twenties, but she'd been right. I would have missed it.

They filed in looking a little weary. Not unusual for a Monday, though most of them weren't big partiers. I had twelve students in the class, and we used more of a conference room than a classroom. I sometimes had PowerPoints for them and brief lectures, but most of our discussions were how most of the information was disseminated.

We had a lively discussion about James Patterson and Dan Brown's use of short chapters and powerful hooks to propel the story forward. Most of them had read the books in a few hours. Then we talked about how much they actually retained and was that a problem in society.

"We're rushing through everything and forgetting to savor the words, the food, the wine or whatever it is we're doing in the moment," I said. "But these authors know how to grab the attention spans of readers who don't normally have one and hold on to it." Then I asked, as I always did, if they had any questions.

The students looked from one to the other.

Something's going on.

Jeff, who was a big fan of all things Marvel—his entire wardrobe declared it so—and was also brilliant, spoke up.

"Lily heard from her Grandma Helen that you guys are doing some murder book club. That you put a board together like on a television show."

Dear. Lord. Those women could not keep their mouths shut. I wondered if maybe I should kick them out of the book club.

"That's gossip not a question." My words came out a bit sharper than I meant.

"Well, some of us are wondering if we could join your murder club. Is that okay?" Jeff asked.

"It's a *book club*, and free to anyone who wants to come to the market on a Friday night, but I have a feeling you guys have something better to do."

"Not really," Lily said. "I mean, we can always go out after. I was thinking about doing my midterm paper on how closely real-life crime solving is like popular books and television. My cousin Kevin says most of the time that sort of stuff gets it way wrong. It might be fun to be a part of something that could help solve a crime."

Oh my, what have I done? "We're not trying to solve a crime. My investigation—" that sounded so weird "—is more about proving my friend Michael's innocence. He didn't do it. I know it, and I think the police know it. But the mayor doesn't like that we had a murder in town, so they need a prime suspect. And why am I telling you all of this?"

"Because it's fascinating," Jeff says. "This is some guy's life that hangs in the balance."

"That guy is my *friend*," I said, closing my laptop. "And I don't know how much we're really helping. The police have been doing a lot of grunt work."

"But it's talking to people, right?" Lily asked. "I mean, would you want to talk to the police? They might be more willing to talk to one of us."

"And put your lives in danger?" I asked. "That would be a hard pass. None of you will be talking to any suspects. Do you hear me?"

The class nodded, everyone except for Lily and Jeff.

"With all due respect, Professor McGregor, we're all adults here. What we choose to do in our free time is up to us."

"Not if it gets you killed. I won't stop you from coming to book club, but you will not be assisting in the investigation. Understood?"

This time they all nodded.

"Any chance coming to the club could count as extra credit?" asked Eric, another bright student. They all were. But this guy was always looking for some kind of shortcut.

The class snickered.

I smiled at them. "That would be a solid no. You guys have so much reading for your class. Keep that in mind if you do want to come. That's even more reading on your list."

"Professor," Lily chimed in, "literature is our life."

There were more laughs.

I shook my head. "Fine. But you've been warned."

"Can you tell us about the suspects you have so far?" That was Jeff.

"It's not relevant to the class."

"Oh, but I think it is," Jeff said. "You could look at it in the way we just did the Patterson book. It's usually the husband, wife or significant other. We've learned that in most of the mysteries we've read. The murderer is almost always someone the person knows. I saw the news reports. Your friend was railroaded in my opinion. His motive isn't strong enough."

This kid was way too smart. I guess there was no way of getting out of this and we did have a good ten minutes left. "That's true but in this case, the two people closest to him have strong alibis with multiple witnesses."

"When I saw that on the old *Castle* episodes the strong alibis never hold up. He had a wife and a mistress. If that's not motive, I don't know what is," Lily said.

I laughed. "But this is real life and maybe Jeff is right. Not all murders are like the ones we read in books, see on television or in films. My brother always says the simple answer is usually the right one and most murders are committed by someone close to the victim. That's why them focusing on Michael doesn't make any sense. He was a casual business acquaintance."

"In the *Orient Express*, they all did it and changed the timeline to make it look like he died at a certain time, but it was all lies," Jeff said.

That reminded me, I still hadn't looked at the autopsy report. What if he hadn't been killed there? For a head wound, not that I know much about these sorts of things, but there wasn't a lot of blood. Or what if he didn't die right way? Maybe he died hours after that initial wound. That would change things.

My brother had probably looked at all of those angles, but it wouldn't hurt to have fresh eyes. What if the mistress really did know about the wife and vice versa?

They could be working together.

But then that made that scene outside the coroner's office Oscar worthy. They were genuinely angry. Could someone fake that kind of passion?

My phone buzzed letting me know it was time to let them go.

"Class is dismissed. Just so you guys know, showing up to book club does not in any way help your grade. Go and have a life. Grad school takes up enough of it."

They were all talking about the murder and one of them suggested they put a study group together to go over all the news footage so far.

What was it about people nosing into murders like they could solve them?

Like you?

Well, there was that.

I prayed none of them showed up to book club.

The last thing I needed was one more person telling the whole town what we were up to.

There was something weird about the wife and girlfriend though.

I needed to talk to them both and it wasn't just morbid curiosity. I felt like I'd know if they were lying to me.

There was no way I could just show up on their door-steps.

Hmmm. Maybe I, as the sister of the sheriff couldn't, but someone else might be able to.

A plan formed and I couldn't help but smile.

Chapter Ten

I'D JUST TURNED on my car in front of the university, when Shannon called. "He's getting out on bail." The relief in her voice put a smile on my face.

"I know one coffee house owner who is extremely happy right now."

"Girl, you have no idea."

I did. I was equally excited. Trials took a long time to put together and that gave us a better chance of finding the real killer before they sent Michael away.

"Was it the lawyer who finally convinced him?"

She laughed. "No. That would be me. I decided enough was enough. I went down there and told him what your brother said to me earlier this morning. That he was going to county and it was not a nice place. That he was being selfish making me worry all the time.

"That I cry myself to sleep. And if things didn't get fixed, well, either way, we need to spend as much time together as possible. Then I cried. Like big blubbery tears. He can't take a woman crying, especially me. I wasn't faking it. Though, I would have done that a long time ago if I'd known how fast it worked on him."

I snorted and then coughed a little. It was a good thing I wasn't on the road yet. "I'd like to come see you guys—not tonight. You need some alone time, but maybe tomorrow."

"Oh, that's why I called. I'm throwing a little welcome home party for him tonight at my place. Just some sweets, snacks and wine. Nothing too fancy. Jake and Kane are coming. For the record, I invited Greg, but he's working another case tonight."

My brother had been busier than ever lately. They usually sat around the station most days playing solitaire or poker on their computers, but he'd been out in the field almost every day since the murder. The fall festival security was a big deal, but I wondered if there might be something else going on. I needed to ask him about that.

"What time and what do you want me to bring?"

"Around seven, and I've got everything covered. Oh, and George Clooney is invited as well. Michael was asking about him."

"He'll be okay at home for a little while." Well, last time I'd left him he'd eaten all the sofa cushions. Nothing like some separation anxiety with a ginormous dog.

George grunted from the back seat, as if to say, "No. I won't. I might eat a sofa if you aren't there to hang out with me."

Weird since most of the day and night he slept. But when he was alone, he was so anxious. And given what had happened over the last week, it probably wasn't a good idea. He might eat the door if something was going on outside.

"No. Really. He loves Mr. Snuffles, even if that love isn't returned. If he's here, I don't have to worry about Snuffs coming out of the bedroom and walking all over the food. I swear that cat is Houdini. I'll be glad when Michael and I are married, and I can let him outside at the winery. Here in town it's too dangerous. And I'm babbling. Sorry. I'm just really happy for the first time in a week."

"I totally get it. And you listen to me all the time, so let's not worry about that sort of thing when we're together."

"Agreed. See you at seven."

After she hung up, I pushed the button to call my brother. It went straight to voice mail. I didn't bother leaving a message.

It was cutting it close, but I decided to head home to let George run around, and, to be honest, change clothes to something more party appropriate. While he did his crazy dog routine, I searched through my closet.

Nothing.

I texted Shannon. *What are you wearing?*

She called me. "I've got dough on my hands so calling is easier. It's very casual. Jeans and a cute top, maybe. Oh, and my new boots from when we went shopping in September. It's just now cool enough to wear them. Goodness, that seems like a hundred years ago."

"It does." We'd taken a trip up to Austin. Me to search for some artists who might want to share their work in the gallery section of the store, and her to pick up some new clothes. I'd also bought boots. I pulled them out. "Okay. Thanks. I wasn't sure if I needed a dress, which I absolutely do not have, or if jeans were okay."

"No worries. I've got to go pick up Michael—they said he'd be ready at six. I'll see you soon."

"Bye." It wasn't true that I didn't have cocktail dresses. I did. But they didn't quite fit like they used to. I'm a bit curvier than I was when I lived in Chicago, and I don't mind it. Not so great that many of my clothes didn't fit, but awesome that I was more comfortable in my skin than I had been in a long time.

I'd bought some jeans and a couple of tops on the trip. Most of the time I wore very comfortable clothes these days. I picked the red layered top. It had long draping sleeves and was made out of a soft, gauzy material.

I pulled on my dark jeans, and the boots, and looked at myself in the mirror.

Ainsley McGregor, entrepreneur. Look at you. Funny what a difference a year made. Even before the incident in Chicago, my skin was sallow, and I was so unhappy. I didn't know how much at the time.

It wasn't until I started working on the plans for the store, that it dawned on how happy I was in Texas. My skin had recovered, and I'd put on weight, and my life was full of people who genuinely cared for me.

Life is good.

So, if some of my clothes didn't fit—whatever.

I threw on some mascara, blush and lipstick. With my red hair, and pale skin, if I don't add a little color, I'm totally washed out.

The party was in full swing when I arrived. They'd invited some of the gang from the market and everyone had big smiles on their face. George Clooney is so much more social than I am. He just went on in and straight for Jake and Kane, who were conversing in the corner.

"George!" Jake said as he knelt down to give my dog a hug. *Lucky dog.*

Wait. Did I just think that? Goodness knows he didn't see me as anything but his best friend's little sister.

"Man, I love this dog," Kane said as he ran his hand along George's back, which other than a chin rub, which Jake was giving him, was his favorite thing in the world.

Again, lucky dog.

"George, leave them alone." I swear my dog turned his head and gave me the weirdest look.

"Did he just give you side-eye?" Jake asked and we all laughed.

"How are you guys?"

"Good," Kane said. "I wanted to thank you again for that lasagna. I don't get back as much as I'd like to Dallas to visit my grandmother. That's usually the only time I get a home-cooked meal. So that was a treat. I miss your brother's barbeques. He has some mad grill skills."

I smiled. Kane might spend most of his days with dead people, but he was a kind soul and so personable. The fact that he was Idris Elba's doppelganger was just a plus.

"What are you two drinking?"

"Something called butterbeer."

"Better watch out," I warned. "That stuff is like crack. She made me some last night. I'm pretty sure it's five thousand calories a cup and I had at least six. I'm grateful I could zip up my jeans."

Ainsley. Hush. These guys don't care about the fact the majority of your wardrobe is tight.

"I think you look great," Jake said.

"Absolutely," Kane added.

I couldn't help but laugh. "I wasn't fishing for compliments, I promise. But thanks, guys. I should probably go say hello to the host and guest of honor."

Yes, please exit before you make a total jerk of yourself.

Shannon was in the kitchen running around like a crazy person.

"What can I do to help?"

"You can find my fiancé," she said as she plated some of her famous snickerdoodles. "He probably just needed some quiet time. But it makes him look—Just find him, please."

"Got it. Save me one of those cookies for later."

She nodded and then plastered a fake smile on her face as she entered the living room with the tray of goodies.

After checking the bathroom and the two bedrooms, I headed up to the rooftop. That was my favorite place to hang out when I visited, and I had a feeling Michael was up there breathing in the fresh air. I didn't blame him.

When I opened the glass door at the top of the stairs, he was there on the first lounger. Shannon had the whole thing set up like a small garden with planters full of flowers and vegetables. There were loungers and tables and chairs. Normally, the parties were held up here, but there was a distinct chill in the air tonight.

"Michael, I've been sent by your fiancée to find you."

He smiled but it didn't reach his eyes. "I was feeling a little claustrophobic," he said. "I just need a minute or two. Everyone who came in seemed so—I don't know."

"Like they're pretending you didn't just spend almost a week in jail."

He chuckled. "Ainsley, you do like to tell it like it is."

I shrugged. "We're friends. You know you can talk to me

if you want."

"I'm surprised you aren't already quizzing me about your murder board." He sat back in his chair and crossed his legs on the lounger.

"Well, you're at the bottom of the suspect list on my board. So, there's not a lot I have to ask. Though, I am curious. If you were out at the winery, surely someone saw you."

This time he was the one who shrugged. "I would have thought so too. There's a whole team of guys who live out in the bunkhouse during this part of the season when we're trimming back the vines. Just my luck that not a one of them saw me walking the vines before I went in the house. The last time I saw Rick Dean was when he walked out of the restaurant. I was kind of embarrassed by the way he treated Dooley. So, I stayed a bit to finish my meal. Then I drove straight home. None of this makes sense."

"There's a good portion of the town, including me, who believe you."

"Except for whoever trashed the barn. Poor Shannon. I think this has been tougher on her than it has me. I thought it was safer for me to stay in lockup. I had this dumb idea that maybe the killer would slip up and do something while I was in there."

I thought about the footprint out at my place. "There's a chance he or she may have done exactly that." I told him about George and what happened.

"Could be hunters out there. Me and my dad used to be up there all the time. Though, it wasn't something I was good at. Could never kill an animal, even if there's an overpopulation. Just feels wrong."

And this was the guy who'd been framed for murder. "I think someone is working very hard to make it seem like you were the one who killed Rick."

"Yep. I might not be Einstein, but even I wouldn't use my own wine bottle to commit a felony. It's just crazy. That female detective, you know, I'm all about women's empowerment, but she has it in for me. It's like she thinks this is some career-making chance for her to close a big case."

"I haven't seen her around the station much, the last few times I've been there. I came to see you twice, by the way. But you were busy with other people."

"Yeah, your brother told me. I appreciate that. I didn't want to talk to anyone there for a while. I was always afraid I might say the wrong thing and you never know who's watching.

"I didn't like Rick Dean. Shannon probably told you, but he was fake from day one. All his emails about investing and all that—lies. He was trying to buy the business for almost no money for the corporation that employs him. Did you know he made a pass at Shannon?"

Oh, so he did know. That could be motive. Crud. I still didn't believe he did it, but there was a niggling of doubt in my brain. "I didn't realize she'd told you."

"She didn't until today. I've been feeling terrible guilt. I mean, I didn't like the guy, but no one deserves to die like that. I kept wondering while I was locked up if there was something I could do. Then Shannon told me what he did. I don't understand guys like that."

Well, there goes that motive. Thank goodness.

"Me either. I do have a question I need to ask, and it's kind of awkward."

"Go for it. Can't be any worse than what that detective put me through. Sometimes she was asking questions for two or three hours, one right after another like she was trying to catch me up. She's not my favorite person but she's good at what she does. A couple of times I almost made something up to make her stop. But about the time I felt like I might, Greg always came in and sort of saved the day. I don't know what I would have done without him in there. I was going out of my ever-lovin' mind. You said you had a question?"

"Is there anyone you can think of who might want to cause you harm? Anyone you made angry and they're trying to get back at you?"

"Nah. You know me, Ains. I'm pretty easygoing. I mean, Rick Dean made me mad, but even then, it was more about me trying to get away from him. I was initially interested in working with his company as a nationwide distributor for the wine and spirits. Rick is a national salesman and proposed some pretty heavy incentives to get me to sign with his company.

"But ultimately, he wasn't a good guy. First thing he said to me after inspecting the grapes, is that he would have done it all differently. Then he went off on everything I was doing wrong. Everyone has an opinion, and I told him so. Said I didn't think we'd work well together. And then he was tenacious. Like he just couldn't let it go."

"But can you think of anyone else who might want to frame you for murder?"

He shook his head. "Nah. I stay out of other people's

business. We live in a good place here and these people are my friends."

He was right. Michael had no enemies, except for whoever wrote that note on the barn. I asked him who he thought did it.

"No clue," he said. "They had to be pretty tall to get those letters up like that. They were almost twenty feet high in some places, so even on a ladder, they'd need some height. They were awful quiet. The bunkhouse is just on the other side of barn. One of the guys would have heard them."

"Hmmm. I've got one more question and then we'd better go inside before Shannon puts the hurt on us both. What can you tell me about Danny Avery?"

"Danny? What's he got to do with any of this?"

"Well, he seemed to swoop in kind of fast. Shannon says he's done a great job keeping things going. But I'm just trying to make sure we've covered all our bases."

"She's right. He's been nothing but kind. His company also wants to invest, but he's been a friend of mine for a few years. I'd only listened to Rick Dean's proposal because he insisted on talking to me. He just moved to the area, so I was trying to be a good neighbor—fat lotta good that did me." Michael rubbed a hand on his chin. "I'd already decided to go with Danny's company. He was working on the contracts before I met Rick. And I think he was in Dallas when all that went down."

Hmmmm. Poor Michael had been through enough.

"Did you have any idea that Rick had a mistress and a wife?"

He shook his head. "I didn't know him well, but he just

didn't seem the type to take time for a girlfriend. He was all about numbers and mentioned a couple of times that he worked sixteen-hour days. And I can't imagine anyone would willingly spend time with that guy. He was so annoying."

He breathed a heavy sigh. "I shouldn't say that."

"I get it," I said. "I imagine your fiancée and the guests are wondering where you are."

He stood and then reached a hand to help me up.

"Thanks, Ainsley, for everything you're doing. And for looking after Shannon. I really appreciate it. I don't know how she's going to handle it if—"

If he went to prison for a crime he didn't commit.

"It's going to be okay. We're going to figure all of this out."

At least I hoped so.

I was more determined than ever to find the real killer.

Chapter Eleven

I N MY OLD life back in Chicago, people partied until the wee hours of the morning. In Sweet River, not so much. By nine p.m. most of the guests had left and I was in the kitchen doing the dishes so Shannon could visit with those who remained. Kane walked in carrying the last of the plates.

"I'll put them in the dishwasher," he said.

"Thanks, I've got it. But if you want to start putting some of the food into the plastic bowls, that would be helpful."

"No problem. There isn't a lot left. People in this town really love her food."

"Those snickerdoodles—don't even ask me how many I've eaten," I said as I put some plates in the dishwasher. No paper for Shannon. She put out the good stuff when she entertained.

"Are you going to the fall festival next weekend?"

"Yeah. Well, I have to work it for a while. The store has a booth full of samples."

"How about you?"

There was a long pause, I craned my neck to look at him and he had a weird expression.

"What? Do I have cookie on my face? I totally stuffed one in my mouth as you walked in. Fuel for doing the dishes," I explained.

He laughed hard at that. "I was going to see if maybe you wanted to go with me and some friends," he said quickly.

I dropped the dishrag on the floor and my jaw dropped, as well. "Oh. Uh."

"Just friends," he said and then shoved some cookies into one of the containers. "I thought as the somewhat new kids to town, we could go together. Most of the folks at the station will be working the festival. But I asked a few of my friends to come down, and I thought you might like to join us."

"Right. Understood." I mean, why would a guy who looked like Idris Elba ask me out? Like Jake, he was so out of my league. "If what you want is someone to go on the rides with, I'm in. Last year, I went with Shannon and Michael and I most definitely felt like the third wheel."

We finished up and were about to walk out of the kitchen when he touched my shoulder.

"Hey," he said, "about before."

Was he already going to cancel our not date?

"I'm really busy with my job."

I wasn't really sure what he meant. "No worries. If you asked me out on a real date, I probably would have said no. After my last breakup, I kind of have a moratorium on dating. But friends going to a festival, that I can do."

His smile was heart-melting. "Whew. Okay. Just—I mean, if I were going to ask someone, it would be you. But I'm married to my job right now."

"Me too," I squeaked out. I wasn't sure if I was flattered that he considered me dating material or upset that he couldn't make that leap.

Way to have some self-esteem, Ainsley. I really am comfortable with who I am, but I'm definitely not ready for any kind of relationship.

So why are you even thinking about this?

Right. But the answer to that was he really does look like Idris, so who wouldn't?

We were about to join the others when I placed a hand on his arm. "I'd actually like to ask you something about work. Just one question, if that's okay."

He laughed. "I'm afraid to say yes. But what is it?"

"How certain is the time of death? I mean, is it possible to get that wrong?"

"Ainsley, are you questioning the way I do my job?" His face was impassive, and I couldn't figure out if he was angry. Leave it to me to offend someone who wanted to spend time with me.

"Of course not. The whole thing against Michael hinges on time of death because he's the only one who doesn't have an alibi. But maybe if that was off, even by a few hours, that could help his case. It would mean things couldn't be proven without a shadow of a doubt."

He gave me a strange look.

"Yes, I know that line is straight out of an old *Castle* episode. I'm just curious."

"Time of death is always an approximation. I narrowed it down to about a two-hour period. I take the body temperature at the scene and factor in as many variables as possible: temperature, the type of ground the body is on, all sorts of things. It's one of the hardest things to determine but we get close."

Well, shoot. That didn't help very much.

Then an idea hit me. Something one of my students had said earlier in the day clicked. "I'm thinking about writing a book, maybe a mystery one. I wondered, and it's okay to say no, if I could maybe come talk to you at your office. Sort of see how things work in a coroner's office."

Yes, this was a brilliant idea. Even my brother might let me snoop around if I told him I was writing a book. And I had been thinking about working on one before I started the shop. Though, it was more a historical idea set in the Tudor area. But writing a mystery did have its appeal.

"I—uh, hmmm. Sure. It's just if you're not used to see-ing dead bodies, it might be more the thing of nightmares for most people."

Oh. I forgot about the dead bodies part. Seeing that poor man lying in the park with those glassy eyes—yep, that was something I'd never forget. But this was what I needed to do to help Michael. I'd get peppermint for my nose to help with smell, and maybe I just wouldn't look too closely. I could do this.

Maybe.

The expression on Michael's face when we'd been on the rooftop, that pained look in his eyes, drove me forward. "I understand, but I think it would help a lot. If it's okay with you—I don't want to be a bother."

"Just let me know when you think you might want to stop by."

"Thanks." I'd be busy at the shop the next few days. But I could maybe get away at lunch. "How about Wednesday around one? I could bring you some lunch and coffee from Shannon's place."

"Sounds good."

"Hey, Ainsley, are you heading out?" Jake walked up to us.

"Yes."

"I'm going to follow you out and show you how the lights work that I set up for you."

I waved a goodbye to Kane, and hugged Shannon and Michael. "Love you guys," I said.

"Right back at you, bestie," Shannon said.

"Come on, George." He gave me the evil George eye. Michael had been rubbing his ears, which was the language of love for my dog. "I promise T-R-E-A-T-S."

He cocked his head.

I nodded.

He pushed past and made his way carefully down the stairs to the car. Then waited patiently for me.

"Huh," Jake said. "George Clooney can spell?"

"Yes. If you say that word outright, he goes insane and does what I call the Clooney crazy, where he hops around in circles pretty much destroying everything in his wake. I didn't want to risk Shannon's place."

He laughed.

A few minutes later, we'd arrived at my place. The back of my property was so bright, it was if the sun were shining at ten at night.

Jake ran up and tapped on my window. I rolled it down.

"Stay in your car, let me check this out."

He ran so fast he was around the back of the house before I could roll the window back up. Was someone back there?

For once in my life, I hoped it was an animal who had made all those lights go on.

And why was I sitting in the car letting poor Jake put himself in possible danger?

"Come on George."

I let him out and we ran to the back. By ran, I mean jogged at a slow pace. I'm not a runner. Even then, I was out of breath.

"It's okay," Jake said. "It was just some squirrels on the fence."

At the mention of squirrels, I grabbed George's collar. He's a great dog, but squirrels are his nemesis.

"So just know that anything can set these off. Birds, squirrels, probably a heavy wind. They're sensitive. It's more so you can see what's out here, without leaving the safety of the house. Greg told me the security guys will be putting up cameras as well, so you'll be able to monitor everything from your phone."

I kind of hated that all of this was necessary, but after a couple of scares over the last week, I needed security. More than anything, I was angry that whomever had been back here, had made me frightened in my own home. It was not fair.

"Okay. Thanks for showing me this," I said, weary and ready for a good night's rest.

"You've got my number, and like I said before, I'm closer. If anything happens or you're uncomfortable in any way, you call. Doesn't matter what time of day or night."

"Thank you, again. For everything."

He headed back to his truck, and I let George Clooney run around like a crazy dog for a few minutes while I changed into PJs.

When I opened the back door, he sat by the back fence as if waiting for something. Creeped me out a bit. I yelled, "Treat," and he did his happy dance and bounded my way.

I tried not to notice that as soon as I shut the backdoor, the lights out back went on again. After giving him his treats, and a bone to chew on, I went around locking windows, doors and shutting the curtains.

For the second night, I sat on the couch listening to every sound until I passed out next to George Clooney.

Chapter Twelve

I F I'D HAD doubts that the excitement over the murder board might die down the week after all the craziness, and things at the shop would slow down, I needn't have worried. Business was still booming, which was a great thing.

Except it was totally messing with my ability to investigate the murder. I had plans to take Kane lunch. Through Helen, I'd learned that the coroner has access to the database that my brother uses for his case files. Not that I was going to try to snoop on that. It would be wrong.

But it wouldn't hurt to ask Kane questions about the case. Maybe there'd be a few things he could look up for me. Any time I had a thought, I'd write it down on a list I kept on my phone. While I'd promised to share things on the murder board, I wasn't about to tell them everything until I'd checked out the clues.

For the first time in days, I felt like I had my brain back. There has been no more scary stuff out at the house the last few nights. I finally felt like I'd caught up on my rest.

By the time lunch rolled around, the place was filled to the brim. Nuts since it was a Wednesday. But word had caught on about us being a one-stop shop for arts, food, wine and so many other things, and we had some visitors from two different senior centers. Their caregivers warned us that sometimes they'll pick things up and forget to pay for them. I've got great security, but the caregivers were at the door searching through bags and pockets, as each one of their patients walked out the door.

Part of me felt sorry for them, but I was grateful they had such wonderful people to look after them. I'd talked to the activities coordinator about sending some of our crafters out to the senior center to teach classes.

Just as I was about to leave, Danny Avery walked up to the counter.

"Hi." He smiled. "How are you?"

"Good?" My tone was short, and he frowned.

Behave Ainsley.

"Sorry, I was on my way out." As if that explained my rudeness. "*And* it's been one of those days." I forced myself to smile. It wasn't his fault I'd had a crazy day.

"I won't keep you. Michael needed me to come and check the stock in the booth. He said to tell you he's sorry that he hasn't been in yet—he's still catching up at the winery. He asked if I could set up a tasting today and run it for a few hours."

See, Ainsley, he's a nice guy helping out your friend. Stop being a jerk to him.

"Oh. Sure. He has a few cases in the storeroom. Let me introduce you to Don, who can help you find those."

I made the introductions and told Don I'd be back in about an hour. He said he'd look after George Clooney for me. No way I could take him with me. One good shake of his head, with slobber flying everywhere, and any evidence Kane might have lying around would be ruined. Not that he left stuff out like that. I was certain he was very neat and orderly.

I half jogged to Shannon's to pick up lunch. She was slammed so no time to visit, which was a good thing. I was already five minutes late. I have a thing about that. I'm minimum five minutes early to most things. Anxiety piles on when I'm running late.

Grabbing my bag of chicken salad sandwiches and fruit salad and two large coffees, I took off for the morgue.

I used my foot to knock on the basement door.

Kane answered, goggles shoved up on his head, his apron covered in blood.

Um. Erp. What was I thinking? My stomach rumbled its dissent about walking into the morgue with food. The chicken salad that smelled so good my mouth salivated, didn't have the same effect mixed with the sight of blood and the strange smells wafting out behind him.

Why did I think this was a good idea?

"Hey," he said. "I didn't realize it was time for lunch. Come on in."

Stomach twisting, and bile rising in my throat, I followed him. There was a body on the table, an elderly gentleman. He was covered with a sheet for the most part. The smell was…not so pleasant. I remembered the peppermint and rosemary balm I brought for under my nose. But my hands were full.

"Why don't you take those to my office? I'll clean up and be right there."

I put everything on his desk. The smell was so much better in here. Antiseptic with a hint of strawberry. A diffuser that sprayed mist mixed with oils was doing its job on the credenza. Even though Kane was no doubt used to a lot of the smells, he probably needed to get away from them every once in a while.

I put the peppermint under my nose, just in case.

When he came back, he'd cleaned up and was handsome as ever.

I sat down in one of the two wooden chairs in front of his desk. The room was sparse. Painted bright white, with a few filing cabinets, a desk and computer. There were a few files stacked neatly in a metal file holder on his desk. He liked things tidy; that was evident.

Wonder what he thinks of my place with all its knickknacks. I'm not exactly a hoarder, but since I bought the house, I've become a bit of a junk gypsy. Turning found objects into useful things.

"This is great," he said, as he sat down in his office chair.

"I appreciate you taking the time to talk with me." I took out the sandwiches and fruit, and then handed him a cup of coffee. "I wasn't sure how you took it, so there's creamer, sugar and the fake stuff in the bag if you need it."

"Shannon's coffee needs nothing," he said.

"I one hundred percent agree."

After we'd eaten a few bites, which I had to force down so I could appear like the idea of a dead body out on the table didn't matter to me, he set his food down. "Feel free to ask me anything."

He was going to be sorry he said that.

I took out a pen and paper so I could keep notes. I didn't usually forget details, it was one of my gifts, but I wanted to make sure it appeared I really was writing a book.

"Tell me what a coroner does."

"Well, a coroner is an elected official, who basically just presides over a body and declares the time of death. They don't necessarily have to have any kind of medical license.

"I'm also a medical examiner, and it's different. I have a medical and a law degree. I do autopsies and investigate deaths. Using everything at my disposal, I determine cause of death. And I do it for the entire county. You'd be surprised how much ground that covers."

I'd had no idea there was a difference between a coroner and an ME. "How many years did you spend in school?" I thought he had to be late twenties, but if he went to medical and law school, he had to be much closer to my age. He didn't look it.

"Way too many to count."

"It's a curious profession, dealing with the dead. I can't help but wonder if there's a story there."

His face hardened but only for a second.

"Or, you can tell me I'm being too nosy and to stick to the topic at hand."

"There is a story. My parents were murdered when I was eleven. That's when I went to live with my grandmother."

"Oh, I'm sorry. Leave it to me to bring up something painful." I couldn't even imagine. My parents died in a car wreck a few years ago but Greg and I were adults when it happened. I still missed them every day, though, and couldn't imagine being a kid and going through that sort of thing. We'd grown to a point where they'd become some of my closest friends and I still wasn't over their deaths.

"It's okay. Their murders were never solved."

I gasped. "I'm so very sorry, truly. More even that I brought it up."

He took a deep breath. "I was lucky that I had my grandmother. Even with tragedy, I had someone who loved me and wanted the best for me. And she kicked my butt. Made me get good grades and it was because I watched mystery shows and all the old ME series that my fascination grew. I think initially I thought maybe I could solve my parents' case, but it ended up being a true calling for me."

"We're so lucky to have you."

He smiled. I smiled. The silence was awkward, so I moved on.

"With the murder of Mr. Dean, you were at the crime scene and then you take all that evidence, determine time of death and how he died?"

He put his sandwich down. "Yes and no. I can usually make a determination at the scene, but I like to do an autopsy, especially in a murder, before saying anything specific."

"Can you take me through what you've found so far on the case with Mr. Dean? I mean, if you're allowed to do that. There's probably some kind of law about divulging that info."

He considered this for a minute and then smiled. It was a very nice grin in my opinion.

"If you were asking about cases in general, and not specifically, I could answer any questions you might have," he said.

I laughed with understanding. "So, hypothetically…"

He laughed.

"Say you had someone who had been killed with a wine bottle. He was found on grass and his head was bashed in. You found the bottle was there. Talk to me about how you came up with the fact that it took a large man to commit the crime."

Because my large man suspect list was very short—Michael—and I knew he didn't do it.

"As I may have mentioned before, the blunt force it takes to bash a skull like his was made by someone tall and strong. I'll be honest, I'm not even sure the person accused of the crime was capable of it. The extent of the victim's injuries just doesn't add up."

"Is that something you've shared with the police? I mean, everything feels so circumstantial."

"I don't disagree with you. But in anger, you never know what someone is capable of. Usually, the simple answer is the right one."

"But, hypothetically speaking, other than the guy accused not wanting to do business with the victim, there was no reason for him to be that angry."

Kane glanced down at the bite left of his sandwich.

"What?"

"There's quite a bit more to the story than you might know," he said.

Just then, his phone rang.

"Excuse me," he said before jumping up and walking out of his office.

"Right. What time?" He glanced back at me. "I can be there in about twenty minutes, if I leave now."

He came back into the office, and I started gathering up my uneaten food.

"Sorry to cut lunch short, but I just caught a case in another town. They need me on the scene now. If you want to stay here and finish feel free," he said as he grabbed a white lab coat and a doctor's bag, or at least I imagined that's what it was. It was a huge black suitcase-looking thing.

"The door automatically locks, so you don't have to worry about that. Unless, being in a morgue freaks you out."

He typed a few things into his computer.

"If you don't mind, I'd like to finish." I held up my sandwich, even though I had no plans to eat it. If there was a stray file about Mr. Dean's case lying around maybe I could catch a quick look, and yes that made me a terrible person. But my friend's life was on the line. No way was I letting him go down for a crime I knew he didn't commit. "If you're sure you don't mind."

"Not at all. Sorry to have to bail so soon into our lunch. I'll make it up to you," he said.

"Don't worry about it. I appreciate you taking the time to talk to me."

"Okay. See you later," he said half running out of the office.

I had a feeling whatever this new case was, he was kind of excited about it. Weird that someone could be so enthralled by death, but after what he said about his parents, he obviously had a passion for finding out what happened to people.

To make sure he was really gone, I ate my fruit cup before walking around to his side of the desk. I was sort of proud of myself for waiting that long.

The computer was dark but when my hand "accidentally" moved the mouse it lit up.

He was already signed into the system, which was kind of complicated, but eventually I found the Rick Dean file. It was exactly as Kane had said, only the photos were a bit more graphic than the ones I'd found on my brother's desk.

Note to self: Do not eat before looking at pictures of murdered bodies. And that was a deep gash on Mr. Dean's head. Kane had not exaggerated.

Um. Disgusting. And moving on.

The police files were a separate attachment. I'd only seen a few things on Greg's desk. Not enough to really help with anything. Did I dare?

Who are you kidding? You're totally doing this. My plan was to just take a quick look and, hopefully, Kane would never be the wiser.

You a terrible human being, Ainsley McGregor. Yes, but Michael deserved all the help he could get. And if shoving aside my moral code a little gave me information that could do that, then it was worth it.

I took pictures of some of the witness interviews with my phone. I was afraid to print anything, and no way I'd email them to myself, even though there was a button for that. No paper trail for bad deeds.

The interviews were several pages long, and there was a note that they hadn't been all transcribed. I didn't want to press my luck by lingering too long, so I took as many pictures as possible.

The last one was Michael's. I did read it, just to see what it was that made the investigators believe he could do anything like it.

The story read the same way as he'd said.

That is until the last page.

The interviewer asked if he'd known the victim had hit on his fiancée.

Michael answered: Yes.

The interviewer asked how that made him feel.

Michael said: How do you think?

Oh. No.

Michael did have a motive. And why would he lie to me about that?

That changed everything.

Not that I thought he did it.

Though, there was a bit more doubt than there had been before. He loved Shannon so much and would do anything to protect her.

But murder?

There was a note from the lead detective. *At the mention of fiancée, subject's facial expression changes, as well as tone. He was angry.*

A phrase that had been mentioned earlier kept rolling around in my brain.

Was it a crime of passion?

Chapter Thirteen

A FEW DAYS later, it was time for another book club meeting. Of course, I hadn't read the book yet. In between logging sales at the register throughout the day, I'd been trying to read a page or two of the thriller we'd picked.

I tried not to frown every time someone interrupted me. This one was a thriller with spies. Man, I love spies. I mean not traitors who are against our country, but like that old show *Alias* or *Whiskey Cavalier*. Being able to be a different person and go undercover. It all sounded so cool.

In theory.

In practice, people died, countries were toppled, and it was extremely dangerous work.

If I decided to actually write a book, I'd make it a thriller. Maybe with a spy, who did things like stop nuclear wars. I had to come up with a fake book idea soon, because my brother had asked me about it twice.

Oh, what a tangled web we weave…

Kane had said something to him and for some reason, my brother thought that was the coolest idea ever.

He'd called me the night before telling me so, and said he was available if I needed any kind of background for law enforcement stuff.

Then he said the thing I dreaded most: "What's it

about?"

It's a perfectly decent question to ask anyone writing a book, unless that person wasn't really working on one. Then there's the problem where I'm not great at lying, especially to my brother.

I'd done a few questionable things the last week but that was in an effort to help my friend. Lying and skulking around were not a part of my character—though, I was sort of wondering about that. If my friend's life wasn't on the line, this subterfuge might be kind of fun.

"I'm still in the outline stages and fleshing out characters," I'd said, as if that answered his question. But it seemed to satisfy him. That fleshing out characters phrase I'd heard from an author who had visited my classes when I worked in Chicago.

It saved me from my brother's third degree. At least now, my fake book idea had a genre. Definitely a spy thriller.

It was almost closing time. I'd thought about going home and letting George do his crazy thing there, but I really needed to read the book if I wanted to lead the discussion.

I decided to take him for a walk, feed him, and then curl up in my office for the next two hours to skim the book.

George groaned beside me. I'd been staring at the back door for goodness knew how long.

"Sorry, big dude. I was lost in thought again."

He trotted out ahead of me, and I held tight to his leash. After finding Mr. Dean, I never wanted George to stray too far in public. He was preoccupied with something in the grass, which was why I stayed on the sidewalk. Snakes were a very real threat in this part of Texas. Though, my brother had said they tended to leave people alone unless they were trampled on. Unfortunately, George was a great trample-on-everything kind of dog. He didn't understand how big he was, so it wasn't his fault.

He paused to check something out, and the hair on the nape of my neck stood up. I turned around quickly to see if someone might be watching us. George didn't seem to notice anything weird. He sniffed the grass and then gently pulled me forward.

Stop being so paranoid.

Some runners jogged past and another guy on a bicycle headed the opposite way on the path across the river.

But the feeling someone might be watching never went away. I shivered again.

When George finally finished his business and had enough exercise, we went back to the store.

On the back door was a sign.

Stop snooping if you know what's good for you.

Bile rose in my throat.

George barked, like he understood it was a threat. Maybe he sensed the muscles in my body had tightened into one big knot.

There had been someone.

I quickly unlocked the door and then shut it just as fast behind us. Nerves rattled and hand shaking, I pulled out my phone and called my brother.

He wasn't in and I didn't leave a message.

This might be a prank. Local teens had been creating havoc for my brother and his deputies. Tipping cows, I didn't even know that was a thing, moving portable stop signs used on county roads, just all kinds of mischief.

I checked the security feed for the back door, but it didn't show anything. I went back a few minutes. And then even more. People from the shop went in and out but no one really paused.

Was it possible I hadn't noticed it when I locked the door? George had been tugging on me, and it was up higher out of my eyesight. The feed for the security only went back an hour—it was a way to save money. But now I wished I'd invested a bit more to have the continuous feed.

I picked up the phone and called the people who monitored my security to do just that.

Then I shook myself as if to rid my bones of the heebie-jeebies. That's what Mrs. Whedon called nerves.

After grabbing a pair of plastic gloves, I went to grab the sign off the back of the door.

It was gone.

What is going on? My hand shook as I closed it again.

George sat still, staring at me like I was a crazy person.

Did I imagine the sign? Am I nuts? Maybe all this amateur mystery sleuthing was getting to me.

"George, did you see the sign?"

"Ruh-ro." *See crazy.* George was doing a Scooby-Doo impression.

When was the last time you ate?

That had to be it. Breakfast. I had a sausage biscuit and that was it. My blood sugar was low, and I imagined the whole thing.

Just to make sure, I checked the security feed. Weird. It didn't show me coming in and out either. That's when I realized there was some sort of disconnect and the feeds for all the cameras were stuck. When I'd tried to rewind from my phone, it had just showed me footage from the last time it worked, which had been earlier that day.

After rebooting the system, everything seemed to work just fine. I sighed. I was letting all this murder business make me crazy. All of this had a perfectly plausible explanation. The system had frozen, and that was why the feed from the cameras was messed up.

Perfectly understandable.

Except for the sign, which I very much wondered if I'd imagined.

The book club folks would be there in an hour. I forced myself to eat the prosciutto and cheese snack I'd brought with me, and then settled down on the sofa in the office with the book.

George curled up next to me. But focusing on the words wasn't easy.

I had a great imagination, but I'd seen that sign, which meant someone had taken it off again in the few minutes George and I had been back inside. And even scarier—it had to be someone my dog knew because he didn't bark.

I shook my head and forced myself to focus on the book.

But dread sat in the pit of my belly like a giant brick.

MY HEAD HURT, and it had nothing to do with the fact that Ms. Helen had possibly bathed in rose perfume. I'd grown to love the busybody, but her scent of choice, not so much.

Well, at least not in the quantities she wore it.

"I liked the ending," Ms. Helen said. "It left more room for adventures in the future."

Ms. Erma sighed. "They spent so much time together, I can't believe she just walked away from him. They didn't even kiss."

Ms. Helen rolled her eyes. "Not everything has to have a romantic ending."

"Who knows what happened," I interjected before the two of them could get into another one of their squabbles. For best friends, they argued like an old married couple. "Maybe the author left it open for the reader to use their imagination about what happened. They could have met later for dinner, or maybe they're already working together on their next assignment."

"That would be my guess," said Jeff, one of my students from the college. "It was kind of a hook at the end so maybe the reader might go for the next book, right?"

I'd only skimmed it but that was something we'd talked about in class. Leaving the reader wondering as a tool to get them to pick up the next book. "Yes. But the question is, did you feel satisfied by the end?"

There were twenty-five people in the larger conference room—even Michael and Shannon had made it. She'd taken him the book while he was locked up.

"It kept my mind busy," he'd said earlier. "She was constantly in even more trouble than I was." He'd said it jokingly, but the laughter in the room was kind of sad. It was his first time back in the shop since he'd been arrested. I didn't blame him. Walking back in here had to be difficult, also sitting with strangers.

I hadn't brought the murder board up on purpose. Mainly, because I wasn't ready to share my suspicions with anyone, and I wanted us to be a *real* book club.

The discussion went on for another twenty minutes and it was a lively one. Everyone had a different opinion on what the heroine was doing next.

We were wrapping up the discussion, when Shannon raised her hand.

"You don't have to do that, you can just speak out," I said, and then smiled.

"Well…we wanted to take a look at the murder board. We were wondering if you guys had any more suspects."

Everyone started talking at once. The stabbing pain behind my eye throbbed just a bit harder.

"How about we adjourn to the smaller classroom downstairs where the board is," I said. "Then we'll take fifteen minutes to go over it. We also need to discuss what genre and book we want to pick next from the list we made, if anyone has a preference, and then we'll figure that out before everyone leaves."

But my words fell onto deaf ears. They were filing out of the classroom as fast as they could.

Shannon and Michael were talking about something in the corner.

"Are you guys sure you want to do this? Won't it be painful?"

Michael shrugged. "I didn't like the guy very much, but no one deserves to die like this. I want to find out who killed him, as much as anyone else. It isn't just about clearing my name, which would be great. I don't expect us to solve the case, but I am interested in hearing all the theories."

"If you're sure," I said as we headed downstairs. I felt bad about keeping what I'd learned from Kane's computer from the gang. It was against the law, even if I did it for the right reasons, and then, there was the fact that not a single person in this town could keep a secret—except maybe the killer.

I was curious about why he'd lied to me about Rick hitting on Shannon.

It was standing room only downstairs, and Don had already taken the canvas cover off the board. The loud chatter stopped as Michael and Shannon entered the room.

The crowd stepped back and he stood in front of the board. I'd moved to the far side of the room. We'd set it up almost like a family tree with the clues we'd talked about under each of the main suspects. There was one name that wasn't on there that I desperately wanted to add, but it would wait.

"My name isn't on here." Michael's voice was little more than a whisper.

"Of course not, son," Mrs. Whedon said. Tonight's outfit was a silk avocado-green pantsuit with wide legs, which matched her eyeglasses. She wore diamond studs in her ears; for her, this was a fun night out.

It is for you, too.

True.

"But I'm the main suspect in the police's case."

Mrs. Whedon patted his shoulder. "Young man, there's not a person in this town who believes you did it. Why do you think we're all standing here? We're going to do whatever it takes to protect you and help prove your innocence."

He hugged Mrs. Whedon fiercely. "Thank you," he said, and then sniffled.

She waved a hand in front of her face as if to keep from crying. I love that woman. Cranky, maybe, but she really did have the sweetest heart.

My head pounded but that didn't keep the tears from burning my eyes. The poor guy probably thought everyone believed the opposite. Even though I'd only lived here a short time, this was one of the reasons I loved this town so much. People had each other's back. They weren't so quick to judge.

It was the very opposite of what I thought small-town living would be.

"All the more reason we should get to work. Anyone have new news?" I asked, though my voice was low and clogged with unshed tears.

"Who's writing things down?" Ms. Helen asked. "Don? You have great handwriting and did it last time. Do you mind?"

The jovial Santa-like man picked up the washable marker with a smile on his face. "Who wants to go first?"

Everyone started talking at once again and I couldn't help but laugh.

Shannon blew a shrill whistle with her fingers, which had George barking from his bed up at the register.

We laughed.

"Maybe we raise our hands and go one at a time," I offered.

Four people's hands went up. I pointed to Ms. Helen.

The woman might be a busybody, but she produced results, more so than just about everyone else put together.

"I'm not supposed to say who said it to me because she could get in trouble for talking about customers at the restaurant." She stared at me pointedly like I was the one who told on her nephew Deputy Kevin.

Wait. Maybe I did—accidentally?

I made the universal motion for my lips were sealed, and I hid my smile because no one was worse than her at keeping a secret.

"Well, turns out the wife and the girlfriend were seen fighting on the street." That was something most of us had either seen or heard about already. "And then a few hours later, Margie, who works at the Hoof (the worst name ever for a steakhouse) over in Crankshaw, saw the pair laughing over a dinner. She told me that the wife paid. And there was no yelling and they were both smiling."

Wait. What? No way. They'd been at each other's throats. "Did you tell your nephew this news?" I asked.

She shook her head. "I tried to, but he told me to mind my own business. Little toot. I used to wipe his butt when he was a baby. Just because I let slip a little bit what he'd mentioned to me—and your brother yelled at him—he's not happy with me."

"I swear I didn't tell Greg anything he didn't already know," I said. "Maybe you aren't the only one Kevin mentioned things to."

"You might be right. What do you think about that news, Ainsley?"

I was about to ask how she talked to the waitress. But she

raised her hand again. "I have a standing date with a gentleman friend every other Thursday there," she said. "Margie has been waiting on my table for years and I'd told her the last time about the murder. She said she'd keep an eye out."

Leave it to Ms. Helen to have a snoop network, and a standing date? I hadn't been on a date in ages—and the one coming up with Kane didn't count. "Interesting. Was there something else?"

"Well, she said later on she was taking a break. When she went to the bathroom, the girlfriend was throwing up. What if she's really pregnant?"

I sat down with a thump on the conference table, which had been pushed to the side to make room for everyone. But why would they be talking if that were the case? If there was any kind of estate, the baby might have a claim. None of this made any sense.

"Go head and write all that down, Don." I wished there was some way I could talk to the girlfriend. I'd thought about taking her a pie or cookies, but I was worried she might remember me from the street that day she fought with the wife.

And she might know I was the sheriff's sister. If he found out I was talking to suspects—well, I didn't want to go there.

Ms. Erma raised her hand. "Yes, ma'am," Don said, as he pointed at the older woman with the marker.

"Well, my friend Mr. Green works at Calworth Funeral Services. I was there for a funeral the other day and he said that the widow had come in. At first, she'd been crying but then when it came to picking out the casket and flowers—well, she said whatever was cheapest. That the man wasn't going to get one more dime from her. What do you think that meant?"

I wouldn't blame her since he had a mistress. "Does she have money or did the husband?" I asked. "Do you think she was talking about the life insurance? Or maybe she was subsidizing him?"

Michael laughed. "Slow down, Ainsley, poor Don is writing as fast as he can."

Maria held up her hand and I realized I hadn't held up mine. "Well, um, my husband runs the bank where they do their business. But no way he's going to share anything with me. I have no way of finding who has the money."

"Is there a way to run a credit check? I mean, if the person you're running it on isn't getting a loan or anything."

Everyone shook their heads, except my student Jeff. He and Lily had been whispering and writing things down all night. "If someone makes a large purchase, there's sometimes a credit check. But I have a friend, who might be able to look into the finances," he said, somewhat sheepishly.

"No. Nothing illegal," I said. "We don't step over those lines, got it? Besides, I told you that your role here is to observe only."

"Yes, ma'am." I still had to get used to people calling me that. In the South, it wasn't because you were old, it was a phrase used to show respect for a woman.

Though, I was probably the last person to talk about crossing lines. I'd done it more than once.

There were a few other comments and then everyone agreed to keep an ear out if they heard anything.

By the time we finished it was almost ten.

George and I headed home. I didn't have to be at the

store until noon, to cover the later shift at the register, but I was exhausted. After putting down my purse, I went to check on George. He was running around the yard like a maniac but there wasn't any barking involved, so there was that. The lights did come on, but for once, nothing seemed out of the ordinary. He ran and ran, and then came inside.

After drinking a bowl of water, he climbed up on the sofa and drifted off. I started to go upstairs, but my mind was whirling with so many things.

I grabbed my phone out of my purse and opened the files I'd taken pictures of on Kane's computer.

When the close-up of the head wound came up, I was glad I hadn't eaten much. I read the notes to the side. Kane said the size of the wound wasn't consistent with breaking a wine bottle over the man's head. *Was not.* So, had he hit his head earlier and then someone pounded him with the bottle?

I read down. Kane had asked the same question.

Interesting.

Still, even with all the new conjecture about the wife and the girlfriend, they wouldn't have been strong enough to do this.

Ugh.

No wonder my brother had his hands full. Every clue just brought more confusing questions.

Grabbing a journal that I used to write down ideas for the shop, I copied what I'd seen on the board. And then added my own notes to it. By the time I was finished, George snored loudly.

My mind whirred with possibilities.

I was so engrossed that when a loud bang slammed against my door, I screamed.

Chapter Fourteen

AFTER GRABBING THE bat from behind the kitchen counter, I headed to the front door. George didn't move, though he did seem curious about what I was doing. He cocked his head to the right.

"Great guard dog you are—why aren't you trying to scare them off?"

"Ainsley? Are you up? I saw the lights on and thought I'd check," Jake said.

I rolled my eyes, and then took a deep settling breath.

After opening the door, I motioned him inside, but he shook his head. "My boots are a mess. That's why I'm here."

Did he want me to wash his boots?

"Do you need to borrow my hose? It's kind of late."

"What?" He glanced down at his feet. "Oh, no. I'm sorry. I don't think I realized the time. I don't want to track mud in your place. Oh, hey George." He held out a hand as my not so great guard dog tried to knock him down with a greeting.

"Why are you here?" It came out much harsher than I intended but he'd scared the crud out of me. "I didn't mean it that way. Sorry, I'm tired."

"My lights came on at my place, so I ran out to see what it was and ended up tracking them all the way to your place.

Then I worried, when I saw your lights on, that you might think I was the intruder, so I decided to come let you know everything's okay."

"Them?" There was more than one person traipsing around the woods in the back of my house. A cold shiver ran through me.

"Yes. A mom and her two babies."

Huh?

"It's deer season. I'm hoping they find safer ground. But it could be what's been upsetting George so much. I tracked them all the way here. There's some high grass that they were chewing on before I scared them. I didn't mean to; I was just running too fast to stop in time."

"Oh. Well, that makes me feel a lot better. Not about you running—but the deer. I'm grateful you stopped by. I have pie."

Why did I say that?

He grinned. "Is that an invitation?"

I cleared my throat because all kinds of frogs were jumping around in there. "It's apple. Shannon's been baking a lot and she gave it to me earlier as some sort of thank you. If you don't help me eat it, I'll probably down the whole thing myself."

Shut. Up. Ainsley. Why did my mouth do this every time he was around? I wasn't some schoolgirl.

He's just a man.

Yes, but a very could-be-a-movie-star kind of man.

He smiled again, and for the life of me I couldn't remember what we'd been talking about. Oh, pie.

I pointed to his feet. "You could leave the boots on the

porch and come on in. That is if you want some. It's the least I can do for you to thank you for running after deer bandits."

Really, Ainsley. Deer bandits.

I sighed—internally.

"I never turn down pie," he said. "If you're sure it's not too late."

"Nope," I said. "I really do appreciate you checking things out for me," I said as I pulled the pie from the fridge, and then the ice cream from the freezer.

After heating up two slices, I held up the ice cream scoop. "One scoop or two?"

"Always two and are both those slices for me?" He chuckled. How could he have a body like that and eat like he did?

"Sure," I said. "Actually, I'd be grateful if you took the whole thing home with you. The last thing I need to do is to eat pie."

He shook his head. "Why do you say that? You have the—guys aren't supposed to say this sort of stuff—but you're perfect the way you are. I like women who aren't afraid of food."

All kinds of warm swirly fun stuff happened from my head to my toes. I might have blushed. My cheeks were hot for sure. "Uh. Thanks."

"That was too much, right? You're Greg's little sister. It's just a couple of times you've said things like that about your weight. I think you look great the way you are."

Sigh. Ugh. Always the little sister. "Uh. Thanks again." After handing the plate with two pieces and several dollops of ice cream, I cut some for myself. "Have you talked to my brother much?"

"It's a busy time of the year for the city," he said. "The fall festival is one of the biggest since it's tied to homecoming at the college. He called yesterday. Said there were some developments with the case, and could I maybe keep an eye out at your place."

"What kind of developments?"

Jake glanced down at his pie as if he'd said too much.

"He told you not to tell me because of the murder board, right?"

He stuffed his mouth full of pie and shrugged. He was good, but I needed to know what was going on.

"There are other suspects, right? Is Michael off the hook?"

I handed him a paper towel, because I'm fancy like that, and he wiped his face. "I honestly don't know the specifics. I promise. But he did say they're running down some leads, and he's having to do a lot of the grunt work because they're stretched so thin. That detective who was running the case is checking out some leads out of town." He held up his hands in surrender. "I swear that's all I know. But he was worried that if someone thinks you saw them… He just wants to keep an eye on your place for a while."

Good shivers were gone, and bad ones were back.

"But I didn't see anything. He'd been dead for a bit, even Kane said so, when I found him."

"Right, but the running you heard, that could have been one of the suspects."

"One of?"

He laughed. "You don't miss much. I'm the fire chief—he doesn't share specifics, even though we're friends. But he did explain enough that he worries about your safety. That's really all I know."

If it was more than one person, the killer could have been hired. But that didn't make sense with what I'd read on Kane's computer. His notes indicated it was a spur-of-the-moment killing—possibly a crime of passion. Killing someone was impossible—nearly impossible. The killer had used whatever was nearest, which was probably why Michael was the number one suspect.

"That's good, though. It means he really doesn't believe Michael did it."

Jake smirked. "Ainsley, we all know it wasn't him. It's Michael. I've seen him stop on the side of the road to help an injured animal, and he's the type who runs across crowded streets to help old women. Honestly, one of the kindest men I've ever met. And I've known him a long time."

"Preaching to the choir," I said. "That's why I was so mad at Greg and that detective."

His eyes went back to his pie. "Lucy is just doing her job."

"You say that like you know her."

This time he was the one who cleared his throat. "We used to date. Uh—a few years ago. But then she decided to go back to school and—we were better off as friends."

Interesting, though not surprising. The detective was beautiful, even if a bit annoying. "Is she the one who got away?"

He frowned. "What do you mean?"

"Everyone has the person who if maybe they'd made different decisions, they'd still be with."

"Ainsley McGregor, you watch too many of those chick flicks."

That made me laugh. "I'm just curious."

"Yep. It's one of the things I like about you." He ate another bite of pie.

What did he mean by that?

"So, you have one of those?" He waved a fork in the air.

"Those?"

"Ones who got away?"

I laughed. "Uh. No. I've been too busy with school and then work. There was a time when I thought maybe I'd found someone… Let's just say, me and relationships—I'm not so lucky in that department."

"Now, that surprises me. I figured you'd been breaking hearts all over Chicago."

I snorted and then almost choked on the bite of pie I had in my mouth. He jumped up and patted my back.

"I'm good," I said through half-chewed bits of pie. Yes, I'm absolutely God's gift to men.

As. If.

"You sure?"

I nodded and grabbed another paper towel to wipe my face and the counter.

"I guess, I should get going," he said, as he moved to put his empty plate in the sink.

"Wait." Why did I have to sound so desperate? "Obviously, this pie is trying to kill me. Why don't you take it home?" I couldn't blame him for wanting to run away. Lord only knew how attractive that had been with me snorting pie crumbs through my nose.

"You sure?"

"Yes. And sorry about that." Just like I said, my track record with men is abysmal. As in, my ex cheated with the woman I thought was my best friend at that time. And that was one of my better stories.

I wrapped up the pie in foil and handed it to him.

"Do you need a ride back to your place?" I asked as I followed him to the door. George jumped off the couch, started to head toward us and then turned. He was much more interested in the floor by the breakfast bar where'd I'd just spewed pie everywhere.

"I don't think I'll ever need a vacuum again," I said.

Jake laughed. "Not with George around. He really is a great dog."

"That he is." I'd give him an extra treat for making my guest laugh after I'd embarrassed myself in the worst way.

"I'm good. It's a short walk if I cross behind the house. In fact, follow me." I did around to the side porch. "See that light through the trees?"

Funny, I'd never noticed that before. "Yes."

"Those are the new lights I just put on my back fence."

That explained why I hadn't seen them before.

"I wanted you to see that I'm never far, if you need me. Just pick up the phone and I'll be here."

He turned toward me and, in the moonlight, his smile— *yep, so not going there.* Even if he weren't woefully out of my league, I'd still be in the friend category because of my brother.

"Thanks again for checking up on me," I said. "And I can't tell you how relieved I am to know it's deer. I've had the weirdest feeling that someone, or I guess something, has been watching me. I know how paranoid that sounds. But it raises the hair on the back of my neck, every time George goes berserk. After what happened to me in Chicago, I felt a—"

"Like you were safer here?"

I nodded. "I guess my brother told you?"

"He did, but only because he wanted me to keep an eye on the guys at the station while he was with you at the hospital."

"You're good at the keeping an eye out thing—and thank you again. For everything from saving me from that dangerous apple pie, to the deer. Be careful." I turned to walk back in the house.

"Ainsley," he said. I turned to find him still standing there. "You are safe. This is a great town. I promise, I'm just right through the trees if you need me. And if ever you get those feelings again, don't be shy about calling, okay?"

"Thanks."

"Oh, and no. Lucy wasn't my someone special." He smiled and then waved.

From inside the house, I watched him through the window as he crossed the acreage separating our places. Then he was out of sight. Knowing he was close did make me feel safer.

But even better—deer were not scary. Possible suspects who may or may not have left notes on the back door of the store—I'd totally forgotten that.

I thought about telling my brother, but it was late. On the off chance he might be resting, I didn't want to interrupt that. Besides, I had no proof. I was sure he'd believe me, but I'd kind of convinced myself maybe I'd imagined it.

After turning out the lights, I headed up to bed.

Desperately trying to forget what just happened, I put some soothing music on my phone and put my headphones on.

A half hour later, my mind had settled.

Right up until I was yanked out of bed.

Chapter Fifteen

I LANDED WITH a thump on my butt. George looming over me and barking anxiously. My groggy brain didn't understand what was happening.

"George. Shhh. It's night, night time. They're just head-phones, and they were not attacking me." He tugged on my arm again. This was a new one. Maybe he really needed to go outside.

I followed him down the stairs and opened the door. Then he just stood there, half in and half out.

The wind whipped around the house bringing a chill. "Dude, don't be such a scaredy-cat. They're just deer. They won't hurt you."

He grunted and turned back at me. Then he cocked his head.

"Sorry. Still can't read your mind. Go potty and hurry up, it's cold." I wrapped my arms around me, wishing I'd grabbed my robe on the way down.

He stayed where he was, but he kept looking back at me.

"In or out?" I used my almost stern voice. Anything more and he'd pout for days—possibly chewing up a favorite sofa pillow or something else I liked. "Please," I added and smiled at him. Though, it probably came as more of a sneer.

He huffed. Went to the nearest fence post, hiked his leg

for all of a second and then trotted back to the porch, sat down and stared at me.

"Seriously, all that drama and I'm not even sure you did anything. Come on."

But he wouldn't budge. I finally reached out and grabbed him by the collar. If someone was out there, he'd be going nuts like he did with the deer.

I had to use all of my weight, but I finally had him back in the house. I shut the door quickly and locked it. And then I turned all the lights on in the back and stared through the window.

Nothing.

"George. Uh." I lowered the sharpness of my tone. "I love ya, big guy, but yanking me out of bed is not nice. I mean, it's better than peeing on the floor, but still."

To avoid it happening again, I shoved his ginormous dog bed up to my room and put his favorite blanket on it. "Stay," I ordered. Then I did the two-finger motion that meant he wasn't supposed to get off the bed.

He grunted, and I swear he rolled his eyes at me.

I'm not sure what he'd been trying to tell me, but he wasn't happy about my cluelessness.

I yawned. "We'll talk about it in the morning, okay?"

He grunted again but did the three-circle spin that Great Danes are so fond of, and then settled down. I put the blanket over him, and he sighed.

Then I stared at the ceiling for the next four hours.

When my alarm clock went off, I put the pillow over my head. But George was at the end of my bed staring and whining. It was slightly higher pitched, and meant he needed to pee really bad.

I let him out the back and made my coffee, thought better of it, and added a shot of espresso. I still had a couple of hours before we had to head to the store, but there'd be no going back to bed.

When I glanced out the back door to see how he was doing, he sat there staring at me.

"George. Come on. You ready for breakfast?"

He lay down.

Well that's new.

"Come on, boy." I rattled his dish, which usually had him salivating. As in, could cover my entire kitchen in slobber in a matter of seconds.

He didn't budge.

Not again.

"No games, okay? I'm tired and grumpy, and I have to get ready for work."

He backed up and then barked sharply.

I jumped, sloshed my coffee on my hand and nearly dropped the cup.

"That's it!" I put it on the counter and headed outside. But as I tried to grab his collar, he darted away and barked.

"George, I really do not like this new game. I haven't had my coffee. You know how dangerous that is."

He barked again.

"Fine. You do you. I'm going to get ready."

I turned around, and then took a step back.

George was there by my side.

There on the siding next to the back door was a sign.

Stop or your next.

The English professor in me couldn't help it. "They spelled *you're* wrong," I said.

George grunted.

The enormity of what I was seeing wasn't lost on me. I just couldn't process it.

"George. Stay."

The last time I'd left the sign on the back door and run inside, it had disappeared. No way that was happening if George guarded it.

I quickly grabbed a pair of plastic gloves and a gallon-sized Ziploc bag. Carefully, I pulled the note, tape and all, off the back wall, and put it in the bag.

I was about to pick up my phone, when it rang. It scared me I dropped it, hit the wrong button and it went to voice mail.

Really?

George came inside, and then butt-checked the door, so it slammed shut. If I hadn't been scared out of my mind, I would have laughed. The sign—that's what he'd been trying to show me last night. And so weird that Jake had just been there.

The deer hadn't been the only thing in the woods.

A voice mail popped up and it was from the store. I hit play.

"Ainsley," Maria said. "Don just found something. You need to get down here quick. We've already called the police."

Oh. No. What now?

I didn't even think about trying to call back—I just had to get there. Less than fifteen minutes later, I made it to the shop.

There was police tape cordoning off the back where I normally parked. I had to go around front.

What happened?

Please tell me someone wasn't murdered back there. The roiling in my gut turned sour and burned my throat.

My phone rang as I pulled onto Main Street.

"Ainsley, where are you?" my brother asked.

"In front of the store—I'm about to come inside. What's going on?"

"I'll tell you when you get here."

The gnawing pit of dread tightening in my belly pulled tighter. I put the leash on George, and he walked inside with me.

There were customers and everyone acted like there was nothing wrong. Maria was at the register. "I'll take George. Your brother needs to talk to you in the back."

"What is it? I need to know."

"Don found something in the back. I don't know what. He told me to call Greg, act like nothing happened so we don't freak the customers out. But I thought I should let you know."

So, no answers there. I left George with her and met my brother back in the break room.

Several of his deputies stood with him. One of them made a motion toward me and Greg turned.

"Good, you're here," he said, his face a mask of concern.

"Just tell me what happened." The words came out terse and his eyebrow went up, but I didn't care. "Has there been another murder?"

That would not be great PR for the store, nor would it look so great for Michael who worked here.

"Calm down, Ains."

There is nothing that annoys me more than my brother's tone sometimes.

"I'm about as calm as someone can get when they've had nothing but cryptic messages about something happening but I'm about to lose my temper."

"There's evidence someone tried to break in, and it looks like your security system has been tampered with."

I crossed my arms in more of a protection mode. At least, no one died.

Mind whirling, I forced myself to focus. "I had a problem with the security feed the other day—it got stuck on a certain picture. I called the service and they're supposed to be out today."

"Convenient. Did anyone else know?"

"Know about the broken security system? No. I didn't tell anyone. I thought it best if no one knew. Word travels fast in this town. Do you think they were trying to rob the store? Or was it something else?"

"Chief, did you want them to fingerprint everyone who works here?" one of the deputies asked. I couldn't remember his name.

My brother nodded. Before I could protest, he held up a hand.

"You have a lot of folks going in and out the back. This

way we can narrow it down. It'll save a ton of time. Okay?"

"Yes. Do you want me to go first?"

"I've already got your prints on file, remember? We did that when you found the body."

No. I didn't remember. I'd tried my best to forget what happened that night. But I wasn't about to admit that to him.

"Right. If it's easier, you can set up in one of the conference rooms. One of the upstairs ones would be best."

He frowned. "What's wrong with the one right around the corner?"

I rubbed my temple. It'd been a stressful couple of weeks with the opening of the store and the murder. My brother seeing the murder board was high on the last-thing-I-wanted-to-happen list.

"Inventory stuff. I'd rather it not get messed up."

"Uh-huh." His eyebrow went up again. "You don't want me to see the murder board."

"Right now, I just want you to figure out who tried to break into my store, which I need to check on." This conversation was going into dangerous territory.

I turned around.

Before I could take a step, he said, "Ainsley, wait."

I glanced back. "What?"

"You said you wondered if they were trying to rob the store, or if it was something else. What did you mean by that?"

I shrugged. "I don't know—something to do with the murder, maybe. Why? Oh, did they actually get in?"

"If they did, they locked the door behind them. Your

friend Maria says that you keep a good inventory of every-thing that comes in and out of here. Can you take a look and make sure nothing is missing?"

Sure, it's not like I have anything else going on.

He's just trying to help.

This was one of those days where the only good option was to go back to bed and start over.

"Yes. I'll check."

It took several hours but with the help of the booth own-ers we went through inventory fairly quickly. Nothing was missing. My brother and his team had wrapped up, but he was still upstairs going over a few things with Don.

Danny Avery was coming out of the storeroom with a case of wine. "Hi, Ainsley."

"Hey," I said. "You helping Michael out again?" I smiled.

"Yes. I thought I'd hang out until he was free and clear. You know, just in case they needed something."

"That's nice of you." And it was.

"Nah. Just doing what friends do." Then he gave me a big smile.

"Well, it's great just the same. I'd imagine you have a job to get back to, though."

I really just couldn't help myself.

"Well, technically, my company sees this as work. I'm helping out one of our clients."

"That's right. I think Shannon told me that Michael was working with you on distribution or something." But this was still going above and beyond the call of duty.

"That's the plan. Well, I guess I better get the shelves

restocked before you close. Have a good one."

"See ya later."

I trudged up the rest of the stairs.

"And when you arrived, the door was locked. You're sure of that?"

"Yes. I had to use my key to get in. Like I told you, I had a box in my hands, and I tried to put the key in, but it got jammed. I jiggled it a bit and it worked. I came inside, went to grab the key, and that's when I noticed the scratches around the door. I honestly didn't think much about it. This is an old place, but then I saw the red spots and I thought it might be blood. I got suspicious and called you."

Blood? No one said anything about blood.

"When you drove up, do you remember seeing anyone else, maybe in the park? There are lots of people out jogging that time of the morning."

"Could have been. I can't honestly say one way or another. It was my first time opening up, and I just wanted to make sure we had everything ready. It's why I came in so early." Don sounded sad, like he felt responsible because he didn't know any more of the facts.

I cleared my throat.

My brother frowned, seemed to be his natural state lately. "Thanks, Don. If we have any follow-ups, I'll give you a call. But if you think of anything, even if it was someone you passed on the drive in, you let me know."

Don started to leave but stopped as I passed him in the doorway. "Ainsley, I should have paid more attention, especially after all the trouble."

Nothing like a sad Santa to break my heart.

"Hey, don't you worry about it." I put a hand on his arm. "I'll be honest, I'm just glad it wasn't me. I'm not sure I'd have stayed as calm as you did, and I might have messed up the crime scene. I'm so grateful to you, and I'm the one who is sorry that you had to go through this today. If you need to take tomorrow off, I understand."

"Nah," he said. "A man needs to work and keep his hands busy. Besides, everyone in town is going to find out what happened, and we might have another rush tomorrow."

I sighed. "There is that."

My brother chuckled.

"You go on home, though. I'm sure Peggy's worried. I'll close up tonight."

The older gentleman gave me a stern look. "My wife would have my hide if I left you here alone, especially with someone trying to break in."

"I'll be here," Greg said. "I'm having dinner at Ainsley's tonight and I'll help her close up."

Don glanced at me. "You sure?"

I nodded and then gave him what I thought was a kind smile. I definitely wasn't feeling it. The last thing I wanted was the interrogation that was about to happen. I so wasn't in the mood.

"I came up to tell you that the inventory checked out. Nothing was missing. Whoever it was probably didn't get in. And why didn't you tell me about the blood?"

"I don't know what kind of blood it is, or if it is. There were only a few drops on the door, and we've sent it off to forensics."

"I thought Kane could do that sort of thing."

"He could type it, for us, usually. But he's working a homicide case in Round Top. We're sending it in to Dallas."

"Okay. Well, you don't need to stay. I'll be fine. We haven't had anyone in the store the last fifteen minutes, so I'm closing early. I think we could all use a little break from the crazy."

"Good. But I'll be staying and helping you out. And I meant it about dinner. We can stop and get some and take it out to your place. I want to check on your security."

"Between you and Jake—he followed a family of deer. Did he tell you? That's what was driving George nuts."

"Yes, he told me. Still, someone messed with the system here. The tech confirmed it. There was something on the feed that someone didn't want anyone to see."

Yep. That wasn't creepy at all. It'd have to be someone with access, since the main system is in my office of the main conference room, which stays locked most of the time.

"It can't be anyone who works here."

He stood, and then followed me out. "Ains, you have good people here. But you said before that area has limited access. It's time for you to think about this with a rational mind. Someone you know, or who works here, could be trying to steal or hide something. Maybe drug traffickers."

"Wow. You just went to a dark place. Who do you think it is? Mrs. Whedon? Maybe the avocado wardrobe is used to distract us. Or maybe it's Don, a.k.a. Santa, who makes wooden animals and has a wife who makes pies and cakes that make a body weep with joy? Or Maria and her five kids are a secret group of thieves."

"I hear what you're saying but even good people make

mistakes sometimes."

I turned on him then. "So, what are you telling me? That this isn't really Mayberry? That some of my dearest friends might be thieves who don't take anything? I get it. You worked in the big cities for a few years and you saw a lot of—I don't even want to think about what you've seen. But you convinced me to come to this town because the people were kind, and loving. They look out for one another.

"And I've absolutely found that to be true. So, stop trying to put doubt in my head and making me suspicious of everyone."

I stomped off, only to stop short at the bottom of the stairs. The door to where we kept the murder board was wide open and the lights were on. I swear it hadn't been that way when I'd walked up to talk to Greg.

"I thought I told you guys to stay out of the big conference room."

"We have the right to search the premises, Ains. There was probable cause for break-in. Besides, the tech was working in your office, remember."

"I—" The words stuck in my throat.

I stood there dumbfounded.

STOP OR DIE, was written on the board, the rest of the clues having been erased.

For some reason it made me think of that old Monty Python sketch: "Cake or Death."

Cake actually sounded really good.

"That's not funny or nice."

"What?" Greg asked behind me, and then I was being pulled backward. "Ains, don't touch anything."

He pushed the button on his shoulder. "Bring the team back to my sister's place. You guys missed something big. We'll be having a chat about that."

"No," I said. "I don't think they did. This just happened. The door was shut when I went up to see you. The light was off. That's why I was surprised. We've been keeping it dark so customers don't wander in and most of the time the door is locked."

"Run and lock the front door right now. I'll get the back. Everyone who is in here needs to stay." For once, I didn't ask questions. I ran to the front counter, grabbed my keys.

"What's the rush?" Maria asked.

I blew out a breath. "Someone left a threatening note on the murder board."

Her hand went to her chest.

"Who else is still here?" My brother came to the front. "I don't see anyone else in the store."

"Ainsley said she wanted to close early and give folks a break. So, we all cleaned up, restocked, and everyone left except for me. I was closing out the register, so it took me a bit longer. I'm scared." She did the same thing I was doing, which was wrapping her arms around herself.

Some jerk scared my friend, and for that—well, darn, they were going to pay. "This is ridiculous," I said. "The sheriff is upstairs, and someone thinks it's a game to write that on the whiteboard and destroy all of our hard work. Never in my life have I wanted to punch someone like I do right now. I thought it was your guys," I said to Greg.

He shook his head. "They wouldn't do that. And except for the security guy, as far as I know, no one else was in there—at least when my team was here."

"We had the board covered, so it's not like a—" I blanched. I'd forgotten all about it.

"What?" my brother and Maria said at the same time.

His guys banged on the front door and he let them in. While he did that, I grabbed my purse.

"What is it?" Greg asked.

I handed him the note that had been taped to the back of the door and told him where I found it.

His hands turned to fists and his face went red. My brother didn't have much of a temper—it's what made him great at his job—but we were about to see it full force.

"Do. Not. Yell. At. Me," I said probably a little louder than I should. Some of his guys were walking past and stopped. "I forgot. Okay. With all the craziness going on here today. It just slipped my mind."

"A note threatening you, slipped your mind?"

I held up a hand. "Yes. Remember there was a lot going on right after I found it this morning on my back door. It was probably on there, the night before. I thought George was playing some kind of game. But—that doesn't matter. What you need to know, is it's not the first one. There was another one on the back door a few days ago—at least I think there was. It was there and then it was gone, when I went to check."

My brother placed the letter on the counter and his fisted hands went to his hips.

George grumbled. Goodness. I'd forgotten to take him on his afternoon walk.

"George, Greg, let's take a walk," I said. Then without

waiting for an answer, I grabbed the leash and headed toward the back door.

"Kevin, tag this and log it into evidence," my brother said behind me. "Then I want you to send it to Dallas. Tell them, prints, paper stock—everything they can tell us, we need to know."

"Got it, Boss."

As we passed by the team in the back, he stopped to brief them. They were dusting everything and doing whatever it is forensic folks do in a small town.

"Talk to Maria. I want to know everyone she can remember who was in the store today—focus on the last hour, first. Then do follow-up interviews with the booth owners who were in today. One of them may have seen something. And I want round-the-clock security here on Main Street, the park and a patrol running at least once an hour out at Ainsley's place."

The other man nodded.

Then Greg motioned we could go through the back door, for which George was most grateful.

"Ainsley McGregor."

"That's my name."

"You're going to tell me everything you know."

I almost laughed but decided against it. He was worried about me and if I were in his place, I wouldn't want jokes.

Just then, George tugged me toward a tree and I nearly bumped into it. That's when it hit me—

"I think I know what happened to Rick Dean."

Chapter Sixteen

THE PARK BEHIND my store crawled with police officers. And half the town was down on the sidewalk. Okay, maybe not half, but a lot. Jake and the fire department had been called in again for crowd control.

I sat with the back door open, just inside the break room drinking a cup of tea. I wanted to close up, race home and crawl into bed. But my brother and his team had set up shop in the back of the store again. And he wanted me to wait for him.

All of this was my fault.

When George nearly ran me into one of the trees down the path toward the old gazebo, it hit me. What if the murder happened somewhere else? My brother, in the few notes I'd seen on his desk had written this down. And it was in Kane's notes about the lack of blood at the scene.

Then there was the confusion over the head wound. Those pictures would probably haunt my mind for life, but it was Kane's note about the head wound being larger than the indention of the murder weapon. He'd gone through several scenarios in his notes, but ultimately landed on the force of the victim falling with the bottle lodged in his head—yes, that had been an erp moment for me—had increased the size of the wound from bashing into the ground.

But where was all the blood? I'd been wondering that since I read the notes. It didn't make a bit of sense.

That's why it hit me that maybe the bottle hit on another tree, or the steel streetlamps, or maybe one of the posts in the gazebo. The first bashing of the head could have been done anywhere and maybe the victim tried to run away.

That's what I'd told my brother.

"Hey, Ains, we're just about finished up. I'll be able to take you home soon," he said.

"Did you find it? The first place?"

He nodded. "It's almost a half mile down. We don't know for sure, but there's some hair in the bark of the tree, and blood. If it hadn't rained the other day, we probably would find more. What made you think of that?"

Well, I couldn't tell him how. Then he'd know I'd very much been doing things I shouldn't, and I already had all kind of guilt about that.

"I don't know. I was doing some—uh—research the other day and it just hit me. I'm pretty sure it's also in one of the James Patterson books. The murder scene isn't the murder scene sort of thing."

"Research? Oh, for your book?"

"I've been reading a lot." That was true. "Different types of subgenres and I guess it sort of stuck with me. You know I can be OCD about details sometimes." That was also true. My mind wouldn't let things go. Like the time I saw a commercial for Reese's peanut butter Easter eggs, and I couldn't sleep until I went to the store and bought some.

And then ate the whole bag. All.

Or the time my ex said his aunt died and I couldn't let it go. Turned out he was on a date with someone else, and his aunt, who I tried to send flowers for the funeral, was not dead.

I called his mother. It was a thing. She thought maybe someone forgot to tell her that her sister was dead. Awkward. It was one of the worst days of my life.

After I saw him in a restaurant with a date, I ran to the alley beside it and cried.

And that's when I was mugged.

I ended up in the hospital with a fractured humerus, a massive headache, and heartache that I'm not sure I'm over. It's been almost two years and it still hurts.

Ugh. Brain. Why did you have to go there?

"Kane's on his way," Greg said as he sat on the stool across from me. "He wanted a first-hand look at the scene. Says maybe I should hire you on as a consultant."

I laughed, but it came out as a weird squeak. "I just had a lucky guess."

"Well, it's worked out. This puts a new spin on things and means we can go back to the beginning. Lucy is on her way, as well."

She'd be the last person I wanted to talk to. "Do you think this means Michael will be off the hook? Maybe it didn't take such a big man to kill him, if he was already injured. Right?"

George barked from under my feet and did the whiny thing that meant he needed a good run. We hadn't finished his walk when I had the epiphany about the case.

"We'll see." He gave George a pat on the head. "I tell

you what, I can have one of the guys run you home. I can lock up when we're done."

I really did want to go. So. Much. Maybe eat some chocolate and popcorn, at the same time, and watch *Mary Poppins* or something that didn't involve murder. I also didn't want to play twenty questions, or more with Detective Lucy.

"It's still light outside. I don't need anyone to run me home. I've got George and a great security system. I swear, with all the lights it's like a football field out there."

He shook his head. "I'd feel better if someone followed you and checked the place out."

If it meant I could go, it was worth it.

"Fine."

"Oh. Hold on, I want to give you something."

He went out back and then returned a few minutes later holding a box.

"I know how you feel about guns, but this is a Taser. You just point it toward the target and shoot."

It looked like a water pistol.

"The wattage on this one is higher than the ones you can buy in the store. It'll take someone out for a good two minutes, which gives you time to get away. Just make sure you keep the batteries charged."

"I don't need all of this, I have George."

He sighed. "I know, but it's better to have some kind of protection for the both of you. Okay. Please, take this and—" He sat a big canister on the table. "This is pepper spray. Carry it with you all the time, okay?"

"There's a hundred percent chance I'm going to end up

hurting myself with this stuff. You've met me. You know how I roll."

I'm not exactly the epitome of grace on a good day, let alone if some bad guy was trying to chase me down.

I shook my head. I'd probably blind myself with that stuff.

He grinned. "I have seen you in action, which is why both of these are incredibly easy to use. Just take them—it'll make me feel better."

I pursed my lips, but then tossed both items in my tote that I carried. "If it means I can go home, I'm happy to do it."

"That's my Ains. After we finish up here, I'll swing by to check on you."

I rolled my eyes. I know—so mature. "I'm fine."

"You received three threatening notes from a killer. You aren't fine."

"Oh. My. God. I just realized something."

"What?"

"Michael can't write. I mean, he can but it's not legible. He writes like a doctor. There's no way he left those notes—they were in Sharpie. Not that you think he did it. Also, he was with Shannon today. They're out at his place, doing their wedding registry online because he can't leave town."

Greg just smiled. "That's all good info. Now, do me a favor. Butt out of this. I don't want whoever is leaving these notes to have any more reasons to hurt you. Understood?"

Technically, other than scaring the wits out of me, I hadn't been hurt at all. Was this gaslighting? Trying to make me feel like I was going crazy? I'd read about it in many books. Someone trying to freak someone out from afar.

There was just one problem, I wasn't scared anymore.

I was mad. Someone was messing with me and my friends.

I wasn't about to let them get away with it.

Chapter Seventeen

L ATER THAT WEEK, the park behind the store had been transformed into an idyllic artsy festival with handmade booths sporting all kinds of foods and wares, carnival rides, and hundreds of people. Since it was fall, all of the booths had been painted in specific autumn colors. The effect was charming, and now that I had a better understanding of how hard the whole town worked to make these events special, there was a certain amount of pride welling in me.

More than a year in advance, each festival—and there were seven throughout the year—was planned meticulously by the city planner, town council, local business owners and volunteers. Every business was expected to contribute.

We kept the shop open but locked the front doors. People who were in the park could enter through the back door and that served as our booth. We also provided our conference rooms for the first-aid volunteers and as a place where police and fire officials could take breaks without having to go too far from the grounds.

The whole river was lit up with twinkly lights in every tree, save two. The one where the victim was found, and the tree where the actual murder had taken place. Those were cordoned off with police tape, and booths had strategically been spaced around the area to distract anyone who might be curious to take a look.

But I knew those trees were there. A murder had taken place just a few hundred yards away from my business.

"Ainsley?"

My head popped up. "Hey, Kane," I'm sure he thought I was some weirdo. I'd been staring out the back door not really at anything specific.

"Do you have time to take a break?"

I nodded, trying to pull myself together.

"These are my friends." He smiled, as he motioned to the couple standing beside him. "Lena and Tyrone, and this is my little brother Kyle Mendoza."

Kyle chuckled. "Man, you have to stop telling people that—it confuses them. His grandma took me in, when I was seven, and this one was eleven. And we are like brothers."

"It's great to meet all of you," I said. "Are you guys having fun?"

Lena nodded. "Is this all yours?" She pointed a finger inside. "It's amazing."

"You can shop when we're done," Tyrone said. "I'm not carrying bags around, and you promised we could do some of the rides."

Lena laughed. "My husband is exactly twelve, which is weird since he's one of the top neuroscientists in the world," she said. "Not that I'm bragging." She hugged him.

"I'm not the top," he said. "Maybe top ten." Then he waggled his eyebrows. "It's my wife who is the star. She just won pediatrician of the year."

"And we don't usually brag like this, but Kane said you might be nervous about hanging with strangers," Lena said.

"Since—uh, you've been through so much."

I frowned.

"I'm just a general practitioner, in Dallas," Kyle said.

"Who happens to be an Ironman winner," Lena said. "Like I said, you're safe with us."

I turned to Kane. "I—uh. I don't understand. What exactly did you say?"

"I just wanted them to keep a lookout for anyone suspicious," Kane said. "Your brother said the killer had been leaving notes and he was worried about you being in public. I just asked them to keep an eye out, I swear." He held his hands up as if in surrender.

Okay, this had gone straight to weird.

"Well, this isn't embarrassing at all," I said.

"I think it's kind of cool," Kyle said. "Not that someone might be after you, but that you've been helping with the investigation. Kane was telling us you had the big idea about the tree."

I crossed my arms. "I thought you couldn't discuss your cases with anyone."

He had the good sense to look a bit chagrined. "These are all medical professionals and I knock around ideas with them."

"It's true," Lena said. "That's one of the reasons why we're here this weekend. That and to check out the festival. Don't be mad at him or your brother. They're just looking out for you."

She reached out a hand toward me. "Come on, after hanging with these guys all weekend, I could use a little estrogen. I don't suppose you know where there's some cotton candy?" Lena asked.

Her smile and easygoing attitude were infectious. "I do. Some of the best you've ever had is just a few booths up." And while the cotton candy was usually my favorite, I had no appetite.

How dare my brother and Kane embarrass me like this. I was perfectly capable of looking after myself.

"I can see those wheels turning," Kane said, running to catch up with Lena and me. "You're angry with me."

I shook my head. "No. More at my brother. I don't need protectors. I've been taking care of myself for a long time."

"I understand how you would feel that way, but your brother—did you know Jake and I were with him when he found out you'd been hurt and hospitalized in Chicago? We were heading out fishing, and the call came in as your emergency contact. He was in shock, and we had to load him on a plane in Austin. He just kept saying your name over and over. Jake actually talked to the nurses at the hospital.

"We were with him when he walked into the hospital room."

I turned toward him. I didn't remember ever seeing them. "You were?"

"You had a pretty bad head injury. When they first called, you'd already been out a few hours."

That night was still in a blur in my mind. My assailant had come from behind and then hit me on the head with the butt of his gun. I'd been lucky that he didn't shoot me.

The crazy thing was, my purse had been found just a few feet down the alley. The only thing missing had been twenty dollars. I'd nearly died for a bit of money.

"I don't remember you guys."

"We left, as soon as we knew you were both okay. He was fine once he walked into that room and found you breathing. You were still out when we left."

"Wow. I had no idea. He never told me any of that."

Kane shrugged. "I'm not sure he remembers much. When he came back home, he asked how he'd gotten to Chicago and we told him. But he'd been so worried—just like he is now. You get it, right? He feels like he's failed you again because someone is threatening you—and this is his town."

I'd never thought of it that way.

"It's the one place he thought he could keep you safe. His pride is also caught up in this. If he can't keep you safe—well, you get it."

"I do. But it's not his fault. I also don't think the danger is from the town. This is one of the safest places in America for a reason—my brother and his team do a great job." I pulled my shoulders up. "The people in this town are amazeballs and there's no place I'd rather live, which is why I'm mad. And I'm almost certain we're looking for a killer who doesn't live here. We all know Mike is innocent, and very few people actually interacted with the victim."

"I got you a pink one," Lena interrupted my thoughts. "And this stuff is made of crack. I've only had three bites and I want to go buy ten more bags."

Kane and I laughed.

"I did say it's the best—and thank you."

"What are you two talking about?" Lena waggled her eyebrows.

"Murder," I said.

Kane shook his head.

Lena smirked. "You should let her come by tomorrow. We're going to do a few experiments with melons."

"Lena." Kane's voice was a hiss.

"What? It's experiments. And your brother told us you were writing a book—maybe it will help with your research. Is it true crime or fiction?"

I'm really going to have to write a book now. "It's fiction but maybe loosely based on actual cases. I'm still in the outlining stages. I can't decide between mystery and thriller."

"Interesting," she said. "I've always wanted to write a book. Maybe more of a romance."

Her husband came up and hugged her from behind.

"As long as it's not our story," he said. "It took me a very long time to realize she was into me."

Kane rolled his eyes. "You've always been pretty clueless when it comes to the opposite sex. Next to Nerd in the dictionary, you'll see a picture of Tyrone."

"But he's a handsome nerd, and he's mine," Lena said touching her husband's cheek.

Their relationship was one I envied, and we'd just met.

We all laughed. We were turning the corner by the hot dog booth, when I saw two people in the shadows of the tree over by the second crime scene. I was about to make a comment, and maybe move a little closer, when the guy turned toward me. I still couldn't see his face, but if ever there was a menacing sense of harm coming off someone, that guy was sending all his bad mojo my way. I could just barely make out the outline of his ball cap.

If only he'd step into the light.

I must have stepped back, because Kane's large hands steadied me.

"Is everything okay?" he asked.

"Someone is near the crime scene," I said. "I thought the police were keeping an eye on that."

He stepped forward, and the guy took off.

Kane chased after him and his friends followed.

Well, I tried to. Have I mentioned I'm not into exercise?

There was a woof as I neared the back of the store. Since I had no idea where they'd all run off to, I went to check on George.

George nudged my hand and I gave him a scratch behind the ears.

"Why were all those people running?" Maria asked.

"Did you see anyone else running ahead of them?"

"No? Is everything okay?"

That meant whoever it was had ditched them back at the festival. He was still around somewhere.

I put George's leash around his neck, and then glanced around. What if whoever that was had stopped nearby? I walked George along the path, careful to stay away from the food booths. My dog pretty much thought everything was a free snack.

I'd only gone maybe thirty feet when I ran into Shannon and Michael. They were laughing about something with Danny. He wore a ball cap, but then so did a lot of other people at the festival. It was Texas. That was a normal wardrobe essential for men around here.

"Ainsley?" Shannon called out. "Is everything okay?"

I must have been staring too long. "Oh, yes. Just thought I'd take George for a walk."

"I thought you were on a date with Kane?"

Dear Lord, could no one keep a secret around here? "Not a date," I said. "I told you, I was just hanging out with him and his friends. Who are super nice."

Shannon pursed her lips. "So, where are they?"

Just then, Danny lifted his head, and a trickle of sweat dripped down his cheek. The guy was in great shape and it was seventy degrees outside. The only way he'd be sweating was if he'd been running.

"Are you enjoying the festival?" My voice was a bit breathy because of the attempted running.

"It's fun," he said, though his smile was forced. It was him. I'd bet my farm on it. But who had he been yelling at? "We were about to go get barbeque. Would you like to join us?"

Yes. I want to know what you're up to.

Why did he run? Or maybe it wasn't him. He'd been nothing but kind.

"We'd love for you to," Shannon said, and Michael nodded.

As much as I wanted to, it wasn't the right time to give Danny the third degree. I had to get him away from my friends.

"Thanks. I appreciate the offer, but I should find my friends. They'll be worried if I don't check in."

Shannon gave me an odd look.

I just smiled. "Besides, George needs to stretch. You guys have fun."

"It was nice to see you again," Danny said. "If you find your friends, bring them along. The more the merrier, and my treat."

Why did I always assume the worst about this guy? He was actually pretty nice. And maybe it hadn't been him running away.

Just the same, I wanted to know more about Danny.

Chapter Eighteen

T HE NEXT DAY, rain clouds were forming, so we decided to clean up the mess we'd made in the park. Kane and his friends had been bashing melons against various trees.

In all, we'd busted up about twenty melons, all the same size as the victim's head. I kept trying to forget that part since it grossed me out every time the juice of the melons spurted out onto the tree.

He and his friends were hilarious to watch, and even though it was funny, they were being so methodical and scientific.

"So, what have you learned from today?" I asked Kane, but his friends were all there.

"I can't—"

"Stop. Do not say you can't discuss this with me. I'm using it for my research. Just tell me in general what you learned about this experiment."

"Come on, Kane," Lena said. "It's not like she isn't in the middle of all this. If someone did come after her, you need her to know as much information as possible."

"It's—I made your brother a promise," Kane said.

I was about to say something mean when Lena punched his arm. Hard enough that Kane rubbed it with his hand.

Good for her.

"Well, I didn't make that promise and couldn't give a hoot about your bro codes," Lena said. "Here's what we figured out. Whoever pushed him the first time, had been at the top of the hill, and he probably stumbled backward a bit, and then they pushed him again, which is when he hit his head."

"How do you know that?"

"Trajectory of the melons," Lena said. "The majority of DNA was on the north side of the tree. That's why we were using the pitching mechanism to throw the melons down. It's tough because you don't know the strength of the killer, so we had to try different pitch strengths. But these last four show that just about anyone could have shoved him hard enough to bust his head on that tree."

"So, the list of suspects has grown. Because, I seem to remember my brother saying that the victim probably fell down, and that's when he was hit over the head with the bottle."

Kane gave me a shrewd look. Crud. Did I just out myself?

Oh. No. It wasn't my brother who said that. It was when I'd been looking at Kane's computer.

I leaned down to stuff the last of the broken melons into a trash bag and started walking back toward George, so that he couldn't see my face. I'm obviously not the best at hiding things.

Or keeping your mouth shut.

"Right," Lena said. "It could have even been two different people."

My phone buzzed in my pocket.

"Professor, you've got to get to the Bar R, now."

"Wait, who is this?"

"Sorry, ma'am. It's Jeff from your English Lit class. I've been following the widow. You'll never guess who she's having drinks with."

"First of all, I'm pretty sure I told you not to do that," I said. If something happened to him, I'd never forgive myself.

"Yes, you did. But I was, um, bored this morning, so I decided to take a drive. I saw her pull out of the CVS on Broad Street, and then she kept going out of town, so I followed. It's barely noon and I thought it was kind of weird she'd show up at a bar."

"I'm not buying the boredom thing and what you're doing is dangerous."

"Yes, ma'am."

"Stop calling me ma'am. And aren't you a little young to be in a bar?"

"Yes, but I'm not in the bar. She met the mistress outside. They hugged, Professor. And I swear they're acting like old friends. Unfortunately, I can't go inside because I'm not twenty-one, which is why I need you to come. Now."

"I'll be there in twenty minutes."

I handed Kane the trash bag. "Um. I have an emergency."

George grumbled beside me. Crud. "George, you're going to have to be a good boy and sit in the car while I take care of something."

"Where are you going? I thought you were heading out to lunch with us?" Kane asked.

"Something's come up. Rain check. Okay?"

Then I did a sort of jog—who am I kidding—it was a fast walk. Thankfully, I wasn't too far from my car at the back of the store.

Twenty minutes later, I was in the parking lot of the Bar R. I was getting out of the car when someone touched my shoulder. I turned, my fist ready to punch whoever was there, when Jeff threw up his hands.

"Sorry. Sorry," he said. "I didn't mean to scare you."

My breathing rapid, I forced myself to take a slow breath. "Never sneak up on a woman like that," I said. "Always announce yourself."

"Noted," he said. "They've been in there, a while. What are you going to do?"

"I have no idea," I said. "You watch George, I'll be back in a minute. George." I pointed to my dog. "Be a good boy and keep Jeff safe."

Then I grabbed my purse and headed into the bar.

The place was clean and had a barbeque place on one side where they sliced up the meat so you could watch, and bar on the other side. I found the two women huddled together in a booth in the back corner. They were so engrossed in their conversation they didn't even notice me.

"How much longer do you think it will take?" the mistress asked.

"No idea. I don't know why they don't just send that big clod to jail, already," the wife answered.

I bit my lip to keep me from saying anything. That big clod was one of my best friends.

"I just want it to all be over so we can leave. We've been waiting on the Maldives for so long."

"I know, Sissy. I know."

Sissy? Wait a minute. How would my brother not know they were sisters? That was insane.

The waitress came up to take my drink order. I ordered a Bloody Mary that I didn't plan to drink and sat there listening.

My brother, I had to tell him.

I was about to pull out my phone, when I sensed someone standing in front of my table.

"You're that girl from the store," the woman said. This one was the mistress—or at least the one who pretended to be.

I gave her my biggest smile. "I own Bless Your Art. Have you come in? I don't remember, though we've been very busy the last few weeks." Thanks to you and your *sissy* murdering her husband.

Oh. My. Was that true? My brain so just went there.

"Yes, I was in there getting some yarn from that—that woman who wears green. I'm taking up knitting."

I'm talking knitting with a possible murderer. Wait. They had an alibi, but I couldn't remember what it was.

"Oh, would you like to join me?" I motioned the seat across from me in the booth. "I'm thinking about taking knitting classes with Mrs. Whedon. She's the one with the yarn booth."

"She's a funny old woman but she knows her yarn. My nerves have been all over the place, and the knitting helps. Thanks, but I'm here with my sister. Good luck with the knitting."

She obviously didn't remember I'd been on the street

that morning when they'd been fighting.

Gross, if Rick Dean had been sleeping with the both of them, but I didn't think it was the case.

They were up to something. Had they murdered him and now were pretending to be his mistress and wife?

None of this made sense.

They left not long after, and as much as I wanted to follow them, I decided it was best if I didn't.

Besides, George had a limit on how long he could sit in a car.

I threw some bills on the table, alongside my untouched drink.

Outside, Jeff was in the car, his shirt drenched with George's drool.

Served him right for snooping when I asked him not to.

Those two women might be murderers.

"What happened?"

I rolled my eyes. "Let's take George for a walk and I'll tell you."

After yelling at him for doing the opposite of what I asked, I told him everything.

"I read a book where they used each other's alibis to kill the other's spouse," Jeff said. "But both of these women had airtight alibis, right? We saw it on the board."

I sighed. "Yes. But maybe they snuck out or something. All I know is I have to tell my brother. He definitely needs to know they're related. The whole mistress thing makes no sense though. Why draw attention to yourself?"

"I—"

Screeching tires, and then a huge yank on George's leash

had me falling off the sidewalk and into the grass. It was a pile of legs, arms and dog.

The wind from the racing car whipped past us and I was so busy trying to make sure Jeff and George were both safe that I saw nothing but a black whir. Then I glanced up.

"Are you okay?"

Jeff had stumbled over George's leash as he was picking himself off the ground.

"I think George just saved our lives," Jeff said and then he stared down at the ground where the tire marks had dug in less than an inch from where we stood. "They were trying to kill us."

The knot in my stomach pulled so tight, I coughed.

"Not us. Me." Did the widow recognize me after all?

I pulled my phone out of my purse and called my brother.

Chapter Nineteen

"THAT'S IT, AINSLEY, house arrest. Or I swear I will put you in a jail cell just to keep you safe." My brother paced back and forth in his office yelling. Normally, I wouldn't let him do that. I didn't take crap from anyone, but he'd been scared. His hands had been shaking when he arrived on the scene, and when he'd realized how close the car had been, he just held me. For a really long time.

I'd never felt so guilty in my life. It wasn't like I was trying to get myself killed. I just seemed to find myself in the wrong place at the wrong time.

"You can't do any of those things. I haven't done anything wrong," I said calmly. "And you haven't answered my questions. What are you going to do about the widow and the fake mistress?"

"Ainsley. No more. You are no longer involved in this case. You'll have a police escort to and from home and work. I'm going to have a squad car at your house every night. I don't want to hear one more word about you running down your list of suspects on the murder board."

"I wasn't. I was having a drink in a bar and I just happened to overhear them talking," I said. "And I don't need all that. You heard what your officer said. Probably someone just took the curve too fast."

Though, even I didn't believe that. I'm pretty sure whoever was driving that car wanted me dead. "And you don't have the manpower to put a squad car outside my house. I'm fine. I have a security system and George. I'm not running down any list."

Mainly because I was fairly certain that one, if not both of those women had tried to kill me. I'd seen and heard too much.

He shoved a hand through his hair. "Just promise me, until I can find the killer, that you're going to stay close to home. Okay? And I will be having a patrol swing by even more often than I have."

I sighed. "You can't do that just because I'm your sister. What will people think?"

"You are my sister and I'll do whatever it takes to protect you. The people in this town will expect that. I know you won't stay with me at my house, but you wouldn't be alone that way."

I shook my head. "No. I let some criminal scare me away from my home in Chicago. I'm not going to do that here. I will be more careful. I promise you. And I have George. Don't forget. He's a gentle giant but if anyone tries to mess with me—let's just say he's got my back."

If it weren't for him, I might be roadkill. I reached down to stroke his ears. He was definitely getting a big bone tonight.

"Someone tried to run over you. Just promise me you'll be hyper aware. If anything strange happens, I don't care if George is barking at a mosquito, you call me."

His eyebrows furrowed, and I was desperate for this conversation to be over.

"I promise. Can we go now?"

He huffed. I started to exit, and then stopped. I walked back around his desk and gave him a hug. "I'm sorry I scared you."

He kissed the top of my head. "You're the only sister I got. I need you to hang around."

I chuckled. "Yes, sir."

Then George and I were off with a police escort. One of the officers drove us in the police sedan, while the other officer drove my car back to the farm.

Once we arrived at the house, the officer who had driven us followed me to the door. I wasn't sure about the protocol and I didn't want to be rude.

"I'll need to let George out," I said as I unlocked the door.

"I'll be going in first, ma'am," Officer Collins said. "I'll give you the go-ahead when it's okay to go inside."

As if he sensed the officer was just trying to keep us safe, George sat there patiently. Usually he'd be super antsy and whining by this point to get out in the backyard.

"Good boy, George." I patted his head while we waited just inside the door. The officer made quick work of opening and closing the pantry and then motioned that it was okay to take George inside.

"I'll check upstairs," he said as he passed us. "Then we're going to do our regular run, but we'll be back to check on you."

I started to say I'd be fine, but it was useless. They worked for my brother and it didn't matter.

George galloped around the backyard like a champ, checking out every blade of grass. His antics helped soothe me. My body was a tight coil of nerves, my stomach so knotted it hurt.

Someone tried to kill me, or at the very least scare the heck out of me. They could have hurt Jeff and George.

The knot tightened. I backed away and sat down at the kitchen table, head in hands, forcing myself to slow my breathing.

"Calm down." I said it out loud.

"You okay, ma'am?"

"Officer Collins?"

"Yes, ma'am."

"I know it's a Southern thing, but please stop calling me ma'am. You're making me feel like I'm a hundred years old."

"Yes—uh, Ms. McGregor."

I laughed. I needed that.

"Are you sure you're okay?"

I nodded. "It's just been a very long day."

There was a woof at the back door, and I stood, on unsteady legs to get George. But it was as if all the wind had gone out from my sails and I flopped back in the chair again.

"You sit tight. I'll let your dog in."

George came bounding in and sniffed my hand. Then he sat and stared at me.

A squawk came from the walkie-talkie on the officer's chest, followed by a voice. "Collins, we have a situation."

I wasn't in the mood for any situations.

George's ears perked up, but he didn't bark. Strange. If there was danger nearby.

"What is it?"

Collins shook his head as he opened the door. "Seems you have company."

Another officer opened my front door and in trod Mrs. Whedon, wagging a finger at him. "It's a good thing you opened that door, Derrick, or I would have called your mama."

Behind her were Shannon and Michael, all of them carrying food. And then came Don, who had something large covered with a blanket, and Maria. Lily followed close behind.

"Um." I couldn't quite form words.

"We heard what happened," Shannon said. "Kevin let it slip that you were at the station and then Ms. Helen, who will be here as soon as Erma is done with her water aerobics, told us. We've decided to have, uh, a—" She stared pointedly at Officer Collins.

"Book club," Don said, quickly. "We're having book club. We also brought you some dinner," he said. "And my wife made you a couple of pies."

I wasn't about to mention book club was a week away. The gang was up to something.

"We've got her covered," Maria said to the officer. "One of or all of us will be staying near her for the foreseeable future. I'm sure you men have better things to do. Here's a care package for the both of you. Feel free to check up on us in a few hours."

She handed Officer Collins a bakery box, and then shooed him out the door.

"But." He stuck his foot in the door and leaned in before

she could shut it. "They didn't say anything about allowing visitors."

"We're family," Shannon said and then picked up her phone. "Greg. You owe me. We're all here at Ainsley's for a visit. Can you please ask your man to stand down and give us a chance to hang out?"

There was a long pause. "Like I said. You. Owe. Me. And if you think I'd let anything happen to my best friend— Right. We'll see you later."

The officer's chest squawked again, and Maria used that as a chance to gently shove him out the door.

"So," Shannon said. "Tell us what happened and don't leave anything out."

I sighed. "Fine. But first someone needs to feed George. I'd do it but I can't stand up right now."

"Oh, dear," Mrs. Whedon said. "Let's get some food in the both of you. You do look a bit peaked."

A half hour later, thanks to some lively conversation that helped me relax, I'd eaten a large quantity of chicken-fried chicken and mashed potatoes.

Don had set up a smaller version of our whiteboard in my living room. I'd made it to the L-shape corner of my couch. Amazing how a little fried chicken put my brain back in order. My body, though stiff from the fall, was more relaxed than I'd been all day.

George was curled up at my feet. And everyone else was stationed around the room, with Don at the whiteboard.

I'd told them everything. About the letters, the car, what I'd overheard. All of it.

"Do you think they murdered him together?"

"They both have alibis, pretty strong ones from what I can remember," said Mrs. Whedon.

Ms. Helen, who had just arrived, was pacing, while Ms. Erma sat thoughtfully in a chair.

"They hired someone," Mrs. Whedon said. "It's the only explanation."

"Yes, but why would they pretend to argue? It doesn't make any sense," Shannon said. "And obviously they weren't both sleeping with him, so why go there?"

Shannon was right. It didn't make any sense. That part of the puzzle drove me nuts. Like why expose themselves?

"And the mistress had been nice, I'd even say kind to me at the bar," I added.

"Right before one of them tried to run you over with a car," Don said, and then crossed his arms. "Those two are up to no good, mark my words."

"They were definitely interested in the insurance money," I said. "At least—I'm not sure. The mistress—I really should try to remember their names—kept asking how much longer they had to wait. I'm assuming it's for the insurance."

"Hmmm. That could take months," Mrs. Whedon said. "When my Harold died, it took them six months to sort it all out. And there was so much paperwork."

"Maybe they were talking about the body?" Jeff spoke up from my phone. He'd called in for a video chat since my brother had a guard outside his dorm room and he wasn't allowed to go anywhere but class and his job. "My friend Eller is working at city hall, and the widow filed a complaint against the sherriff because he won't allow the medical examiner to release the body."

"That's not what I heard," Ms. Erma chimed in. "In light of new evidence, the medical examiner is the one who refuses to release the body."

Ms. Helen gave her a strange look. "And I'm just hearing about this now, Erma?"

The other woman shrugged. "You didn't ask. And Ainsley asked us to keep the details mum unless we were all together."

I had to bite my lip to keep from laughing. Oh, how I adored these people. Yes, they were curious about the case. But they'd also taken excellent care of me.

When I'd been mugged in Chicago, no one, not even the other professors at the university or the dean, had come by to see me. Some had sent cards and flowers, but no one visited. I was lucky to be in this place.

I hadn't felt like I fit in at first, but I did now. I wouldn't give this up for anything and no one was scaring me away from this place.

"So, they hired someone to kill him and are promising to split the insurance. Seems open and shut to me," Michael said. He'd been sitting in the big armchair by the window staring out into the woods.

"Except for the alibis," Jeff added.

Michael sighed. "Except for that."

"Honey, they know you didn't do it. You were at the diner when Ainsley was run off the road. That's got to prove something."

"That and we know the bottle was an afterthought," I said.

Michael frowned. "How'd they get the bottle? We

weren't open yet. So that means it would have been someone who visited the winery, right?" He turned his head toward Shannon, who was seated on the arm of his chair. "Maybe we should go over the receipts from that day."

She patted his arm. "I did. Unfortunately, a lot of them were for cash. There were only a few credit cards run. And don't forget, they sell your wine at the Stop and Shop, and McClean's grocery."

He rubbed the bridge of his nose. "But it seems odd that it would be my bottle of wine, right? When whoever it was could have picked anything?"

"You're right," I said. "That is an odd coincidence. And Michael, I assure you, the police will now have loads more suspects. My brother and Lucy are following several leads. They know you didn't do it."

There was one suspect I couldn't put on the board while Shannon and Michael were there.

I yawned.

"You should get some rest," Mrs. Whedon said. "Soak in some Epsom salts tonight to help with those sore bones and bruises. It helps. I should know. I don't know if you've noticed, but I'm old."

Everyone chuckled. She really was a dear.

Most of the group filed out and I hung up on Jeff, who was nodding off anyway. Poor kid.

The guilt weighed so heavy on me; I was willing to give him a pass on the paper due tomorrow. He deserved a bit of a break, even if he'd been irresponsible following the widow and the mistress.

But you wouldn't know what you do now.

Michael let George out for his nightly romp, and Shannon, who wouldn't let me help, put everything away and cleaned up the kitchen.

"I wish you'd let us stay with you tonight, at least," Shannon said.

"Nah. You guys go home and get some rest. You've both been through so much. I'm fine. The patrol officers will be back soon, and I've got George."

As much as I loved my friends, I needed some alone time.

My dog bounced inside, did his three-circle thing on the end of the couch, and then plopped down.

"Well, he's done for the night." Michael chuckled.

"I think we both are," I said. "Thank you, guys, for coming to hang out. I really appreciate it."

Shannon stood near the couch.

"What?"

She leaned down and hugged me tight. "I don't know what I'd do if something happened to you," she said. Then she let go.

My eyes burned with unshed tears and I sniffled. "I feel the same way about you." I hugged her hard.

"I feel guilty for getting you mixed up in this," she sniffed, and her eyes were shiny with tears.

I shook my head. "You didn't do anything. I'm the one who wanted to help my friends and I'm glad I did."

"I'm always going to owe you one, Ainsley." Michael reached down for an awkward hug. "Thank you for everything."

"Guys, stop it. You would do the same for me."

"You know it," Michael said to her. "You holler if you need anything, okay?" He helped Shannon into her light-weight coat.

"Thanks for everything." I waved and they were off. I should have stood at the door, but I was honestly too tired to get off the couch.

My phone buzzed with a text.

I've got someone heading out to watch the house tonight. Get some sleep.

It was from my brother.

Maybe it was knowing someone would be watching the house, or the exhaustion from the day, but the couch seemed just fine for a little nap.

George's light snore meant he concurred.

I did force myself to turn the lamp off and then I pulled one of the soft blankets I'd bought at the shop over me.

Chapter Twenty

GEORGE BARKED. AND I sat straight up on the couch, rubbing my neck.

Someone ran across my porch. And then there was a big clunk. I was already dialing 911 when Jake yelled, "If you're awake, it's just me. Thought I saw something on the side of the house."

I put my phone down and headed to the front door. "Jake?"

He waved from the other side of the porch. "Sorry. I didn't mean to wake you. There was a shadow, more of blob. Probably just a raccoon but I thought I'd check it out."

"What are you doing here?" My voice was raspy from sleep. And my brain wasn't exactly functioning.

"I was, uh, out in my truck. I've got first watch tonight."

I wrapped my arms around myself. "First watch?"

"Kane and I volunteered to help out. There was something going on at the college tonight and it was all hands on deck. So. Uh. Yep. I really didn't mean to wake you."

"Well, it's silly for you to sit out in the cold. At least, come inside where it's warm."

I rubbed my arms, as the chilly wind bit through my T-shirt. My hair whipped around my face, and I'm sure I looked like something out of a horror film, or one of those people on the news who just found out their neighbor was a serial killer.

Now there's a dark thought.

"Come on inside. You can share the couch with George, and I'll go up to my room. I was getting a crick in my neck anyway."

"Are you sure?" He gave me one of those devastating smiles of his. He was dressed in a Henley and a dark pair of jeans—and of course he looked like he'd just stepped out of the pages of a magazine.

It's not fair.

"Okay. Let me grab some things from my truck."

George hadn't bothered to get up.

"What a great guard dog you are." I gave him an eyebrow, but he just sighed.

He always seemed to know my friends, even by their cars or trucks, and didn't bark like he did when strangers were around.

I stood there a minute waiting for Jake, but he didn't come inside. Wondering if he'd changed his mind, I opened the door.

"Jake?"

Nothing but the wind.

I stepped across the porch, and was about to head toward his truck, when I saw him. "Jake!"

He was facedown on the ground by the driver's side. "Are you okay?" I moved next to him. But it was so dark I couldn't see anything. That's when I realized the porch lights should have come on.

He didn't move or answer. Maybe he'd tripped and hit

his head. George must have heard my cry and came to investigate. He started growling.

"It's just Jake," I said. "He's hurt."

I took a step back. I needed help and my phone.

A figure appeared from the other side of the truck.

I maybe ran backward faster than I ever had in my life when the two-by-four being held by the figure wearing the hoodie came into view. I tried to grab George's collar, but he bounded away, going after the figure, growling and snapping.

The prowler threatened him with the board, but George was having none of it.

It would do me no good to go after the stranger without a weapon. I had to do something. I ran for the door, determined to get the Taser my brother had given me and wishing I'd had time to practice.

I say that, but everything was a blur and slow motion at the same time. I found my purse just as the door slammed behind me. My hand hit the pepper spray first.

"I don't know who you are, but the police are on the way."

George pawed and barked against the door.

At least, he was okay.

"I didn't want to hurt you," he said. I didn't recognize the voice. "I didn't want to hurt anyone. It was an accident."

He stood by the door for a minute, and then brandished the board. "But you know. I could see it in your eyes the other night. I don't know how you figured it out, but you did."

Keep him talking. If he's doing that, he isn't killing me.

At least not yet.

"What do I know?"

"That I killed that little weasel. It started out as just an argument and then the idiot tripped. Threatened to go to the police, or worse, tell Mike what I'd done."

Crud. I did recognize the voice.

Danny. Oh. My.

I was desperately trying to get the lid off the stupid pepper spray, and that's when I realized it had a plastic wrapper around it.

Great. Just great. If I went for my purse again, he'd know.

My best bet was to play stupid.

"I have no idea what you're talking about. Who are you?"

He shook his head. "Ainsley, you're a smart woman. It's what's going to get you killed. Don't play games."

Killed. That was a very scary word.

Run, my brain ordered but my feet wouldn't move.

Come on. Don't be one of those stupid women who just stand there waiting to die.

Run.

He advanced, and I turned. I was halfway to the kitchen when he grabbed the hem of my T-shirt and yanked me back.

Everything my brother taught me kicked in. Instep. Elbow. Kick back to the knee.

There was an oomph and the two-by-four fell to the floor. I tried to pull free, but somehow, he still held on to my shirt.

"I'm going to kill you."

George's barks were deafening.

The last thoughts running through my head were I'd probably need to paint the door thanks to his claws—if I didn't die.

And if that happened, what would this jerk do to George and poor Jake?

He loosened his grip for a few seconds, and I turned and shoved the heel of my hand into his nose. There was a loud crack. With the other hand, I whacked him in the head with the humongous can of pepper spray.

The bat was by the back door, and I had a plan.

But before I could move, Danny stumbled. Blood spurted all over my floors from his face, but his head was up as he tried to staunch the flow. He reached blindly for me, but I danced out of the way. After kicking the board across the room so he couldn't find it, I ran for the bat.

The front door opened, and George ran in like demons were on his tail and took Danny down hard. Then he proceeded to sit on him. Growling so menacingly, I worried he might eat the horrible man's face.

"Get off me, you stupid mutt."

"Stay," Jake yelled from the door. Behind him flashing lights lit up the night sky.

"You okay?" Jake asked. He didn't look so steady on his feet.

"Yes, but you don't look so good."

"I've been better," he said and slid down the wall just inside the entry. "Cavalry's here. You're safe."

"Ainsley!" my brother shouted.

"I'm okay," I yelled back. He ran in and flipped on the light. We all winced.

He might have smiled just a bit when he saw George sitting on Danny Avery. A bit. Then his eyes were on me.

"Are you really okay?"

I nodded, not trusting my voice.

His men surrounded Danny and George.

"Ma'am, I mean Ms. McGregor, can you remove your dog from the suspect?" the officer who had been inside earlier asked.

"He's not a suspect," I said. "He confessed to the murder and he tried to kill me, Jake and George."

There was a long pause.

When the men tried to move George, he growled. Not as mean as he was with Danny, but it was a far from pleasant sound.

"George. Come on, boy. I have a huge bone for you."

He stared at me, and then glanced down. He bared his teeth and growled again.

"Good boy, George. Now come on. Let's get a t-r-e-a-t."

Danny was strangely quiet during all of this. Of course, having a two-hundred-pound dog on his chest was probably making it tough to breathe.

George growled one more time and then padded over to me. After giving me a good sniff, he licked my hand and sat at my feet.

I melted.

My arms wrapped around his neck and I squeezed. Barely holding my tears back.

I didn't look up as they dragged Danny out of my house,

reading him his rights as they did.

"Why does George get all the treats? I opened the door," Jake said.

"Oh, Jake. Your poor head." I let go of George and was headed his way, when the paramedics walked in.

"They need to check you out," Greg said to the both of us.

"I'm fine," I said. My shaking hands betrayed me. "Really. He only got hold of my shirt. It's poor Jake who needs help."

Jake did a swirly thing with his finger. "I saved the day. I opened the door."

My brother shook his head, but he was smiling. "He might have a concussion."

"Yep," I said.

We stood there for a minute and then my brother hugged me hard.

"How did you guys get here so fast?"

"You called 911, but you didn't hang up your phone. Everything was recorded, including, probably, Danny's confession. When I tried to call Jake and he didn't answer— let's just say we all may have broken some land speed records. My truck may need a new engine."

"I used the pepper spray," I said softly. Grateful that I had a brother who loved me so much he would risk his precious truck for me.

"You did?"

My brother glanced down at the floor where the unopened spray sat.

"Conked him on the head. After, I used those moves you

taught me. You saved my life tonight," I said.

"Still here. Really did open the door so George could attack," Jake waved his hand. The paramedics were shining lights in his eyes and he had a dazed look. "Drug myself up the stairs and everything," Jake said. But he was smiling. Wincing and smiling.

"Yes, so many heroes. I'm a lucky woman."

George nudged my hand. "Oh, I promised this one something special. I assume you're going to have to process this crime scene. I should probably put coffee on for everyone."

"Ainsley." My brother pulled me into another hard hug. For a few seconds there, I couldn't breathe.

"I'm okay."

"I know. No more snooping. Okay?"

"Mmmhmmm."

"I really deserve some pie," Jake said.

My brother and I chuckled.

"You need to go to a hospital," Greg said.

"Nah. Just a bump on the head. I know the widows were here earlier. Did they leave pie?"

I nodded. The guy never stopped thinking about food. I kind of liked that about him.

Things would get back to normal someday.

I was really looking forward to that day.

Epilogue

THE GOSSIPERS WERE out in full force on Tuesday when we reopened the shop and once again people brought food and wanted to hear what happened. I ended up going to the back and working on inventory in my office.

I'll be honest, I had no business being at work. I was going through the motions, but I was still in shock. George nudged my hand and I decided some fresh air would do us both some good.

After grabbing his leash, we headed outside, and then I promptly returned for my sweater. The November air was crisper than usual. Nothing like a Chicago winter, but the chill helped clear away the cobwebs in my brain.

We made it to the tree where I'd found the body, and I shivered. Never. I never wanted to see something like that again.

"Ainsley," it was Michael and Shannon. "Are you okay?" Shannon asked.

People had been asking me that a lot. And I'd say fine, but I wasn't. "I'm getting there," I said. "How about you guys?"

"We just came from the police station," Michael said. "They had some questions about, well, you know. I—I can't thank you enough. Everything you did for me, and then, what he put you through. Can you forgive me?" There was a deep gruffness in his voice.

"What? There's nothing to forgive. All you did was trust someone to have your back." I put a hand on his arm. "I love the both of you like family. I'd do anything for you. And his actions have nothing to do with you. He was tricking us all. Do you know why he did it?"

"Your brother wouldn't tell us anything. Said it was an ongoing investigation, just that Michael was in the clear and Danny made a full confession."

I nodded. "You did not hear it from me, but the murder started out as an accident," I told them. "They were arguing over your business. I don't know all the details, but neither one of them had your best interests at heart. Danny was trying to trick you. He was up for some sort of promotion and it wasn't about investing, it was acquiring. They were both trying to buy your winery, not just invest. I guess the upside to all of this, is whatever you're doing is working. Everyone seems to want a piece."

Shannon blew out a breath. "Are there any good people left in the world?"

I smiled. "You guys."

"And you," she said.

"So what about the widow and the sister?" Michael asked.

"Well, that's a whole different story. Turns out the widow forged the husband's signature on several life insurances policies. And if Danny hadn't killed Rick Dean, he probably didn't have many days left. They found cyanide in her house. She and her sister will be going to jail for fraud, probably for a long time. The widow was the one who tried to run me down. She was worried I'd put two and two together. Her tires were a match. The sister wasn't pregnant—they had their wires crossed on who was going to claim the body. The sister thought the widow had already left. It was a big mess they tried to cover."

"Wow." Shannon reached out and pulled me into a hug. "But I don't understand why Danny went after you. I mean, we were all writing things on the murder board. Did he leave those notes?"

I nodded. "There was something about him from the very beginning. He knew I was asking a lot of questions. When he was at the shop, he saw the board. I guess he panicked and thought if he scared me, I might stop."

"But you didn't, and you almost got yourself killed." I jumped as that voice had come from behind me.

I turned to find Jake smiling.

Even with a black eye and bandage around his head, he was glorious.

"I was coming to see you at the hospital later," I said. "Shouldn't you be in bed?"

He gave me that Jake shrug. "They let me out last night. I wanted to check on you and, um, George to see how you're doing. I'm surprised you're back at work. I stopped by the house first."

George had moved away from me to love on Jake. I didn't blame him.

"I couldn't sit at home; I needed to keep busy." It was true. Even though my house was back in order, and I was no longer afraid to be there, I found myself needing to be around people. Or, at least in close proximity. I hadn't planned on half the town showing up to ask me questions.

I didn't mind sharing with these guys, as they'd all been involved as deeply as I had. But I wasn't about to tell the story over and over.

"I'd ask if you're okay, but everyone keeps asking me that and it gets annoying."

Shannon and Michael laughed behind me.

"It does. Why don't you guys come back to the store with me? I have enough food to feed the four of us for months, possibly years."

"I can always eat," Jake said.

"Me too," Michael said.

Shannon and I shared a look. It was this sort of thing I needed. Just hanging out with my friends. Someday I wouldn't wake up with nightmares about being attacked.

Someday.

I had to trust that.

This town, and the people here, well they were my world now.

And there was no place I'd rather be.

The End

If you enjoyed this book, please leave a review at your favorite online retailer! Even if it's just a sentence or two it makes all the difference.

Thanks for reading *A Case for the Winemaker* by Candace Havens!

Discover your next romance at TulePublishing.com.

TULE
PUBLISHING

If you enjoyed *A Case for the Winemaker,*
you'll love the next book in….

The Ainsley McGregor series

Book 1: *A Case for the Winemaker*

Book 2: *A Case for the Yarn Maker*
Coming March 2020!

If you enjoyed *A Case for the Winemaker*,
you'll love Tule's other mystery books!

Slay Bells Ring
by Nancy Robards Thompson

Goode Over Evil
by Leslie Marshman

Bitter Roots
by C.J. Carmichael

About the Author

Bestselling and award-winning author Candace Havens has had more than thirty novels published. She is one of the nation's leading entertainment journalists and has interviewed countless celebrities from George Clooney to Chris Pratt. She does film reviews on Hawkeye in the Morning on 96.3 KSCS.

Visit her website at candacehavens.com

Thank you for reading

A Case for the Winemaker

If you enjoyed this book, you can find more from all our great authors at TulePublishing.com, or from your favorite online retailer.

Printed in Great Britain
by Amazon

49841151R00135